he Parliament House Press Edition, June 2019

Copyright ©2019 by Nicole Knapp

HOOK & CROWN

All rights reserved. Published in the United States by
The Parliament House, a division of Machovi Productions Inc.,
Florida.

This is a work of fiction. Names, characters, places, and incidents are either the product of the author's imagination or are used fictitiously. Any resemblance to actual persons, living or dead, events, or locales is entirely coincidental.

ISBN: 978-1-956136-65-4

Except for the use of any review, the reproduction or utilization of this work, in whole or in part, in any form by any electronic, mechanical, or other means now known or hereafter invented, are forbidden without the written permission of the publisher.

Cover & Interior Design by
Shayne Leighton

Edited by
Hannah Simmons and Jackie Turner

Published by Parliament House Press
www.parliamenthousepress.com

NICOLE KNAPP

PROLOGUE

High above London, a boy with strange green eyes perches on a throne of deep grey rainclouds, twirling a stunning jeweled dagger in his hands. He scans the ground until a familiar girl walks out of the busy airport. He perks up, the dagger forgotten, and watches her. The gusting wind catches her auburn hair, whipping it around her face. Even from the height of the clouds, he can tell that she is beautiful. But he already knows that, of course. This isn't the first time he's laid eyes on her.

The girl walks a few steps and suddenly stops, a lost look marring her lovely features. The boy wonders what she is thinking that could make her stop in her tracks. Far below, the girl tips her chin to the sky. The boy ducks, afraid she might spot him.

But no, her eyes are closed. The girl shakes her head and presses on through the rain. The boy watches her as she climbs into one of the black cars waiting at the curb. Only when the car pulls out of the lot does the boy turn his green gaze to the sky and rocket up into the stars.

ONE

The moment I step out of the airport, I'm slapped in the face by an icy, pelting rain. Everyone always says that it rains constantly in London, but I hadn't actually believed it until right now. After all, people say lots of things that aren't true. That aliens and fairies and ghosts exist, that they saw a vision of Jesus in their soup, that they love you… but it's never true.

Speaking of love—*screw* love. I have come to the conclusion that love doesn't exist. Love is just a marketing ploy to help sell jewelry and gifts that boost sales around holidays. That's how I ended up here, in London. Fleeing from yet another failed relationship, another broken heart. I have a bad habit of falling hard and fast, and I really know how to pick them, let me tell you. The last guy, the straw that broke the camel's back, was the worst of them all. He drew me in with his good looks and his pretty words, but it was all a sham. Isn't it always?

On one of my last nights in my old boarding school, in the dorm room I shared with my now ex-best friend, I walked in after a particularly long and boring study session to find them naked, writhing around on the floor together in front of the little fake Christmas tree she and I had picked out. Stupid me. I actually thought she was my friend, and I let myself believe that he was different. But none of them are different. They all want one thing, and once they get it: *game over.*

I can't count how many times it's happened to me, in one way or another. But it all begins and ends the same: with me running away when my heart shatters into a million tiny fragments. Each time I manage to dust myself off and get back up, superglue the pieces of my heart back together and start over somewhere new. But it felt like pieces went missing every time. Like they were lost to whatever jerk shattered it. And now, my heart is no longer whole. I knew I had to run again, farther this time, away from Oregon, away from the United States. Honestly, I was afraid that if I didn't get away, there'd be nothing left of me to give to the right guy. If he ever shows up...

Another blast of freezing wind and rain in my face shakes me from my thoughts. I look around at my surroundings. The airport behind me is decorated for Christmas, practically screaming with joy and excitement. The people inside are all bustling around, welcoming visitors for the holiday, or departing to wherever they plan to spend it. They all look so happy and warm, but all I feel is cold on the outside and numb on the inside. Sure, it'll be nice to spend Christmas in London. And yes, it is beautiful. But it won't be quite the same without anyone to spend it with.

Alright, maybe I'm being a little bit dramatic. My Great-Uncle Henry lives here. He's the headmaster of the school I'll be attending from now on. I could have come to London to live with him years ago, right after my parents died. But I was so against the idea as a five-year-old that he agreed to pay for me to stay in the States and attend any boarding school that I chose. The invitation to come to London was always open.

Now, twelve years later, I'm finally taking him up on his offer. I've always prided myself on my independence, but this time… it feels different. When I called my Great-Uncle Henry a few nights ago, a total mess, begging to come to London, he didn't hesitate. He bought me a plane ticket the next morning, and now here I am.

That makes me feel a bit better. At least at the new school I can start fresh. I will make new friends, and meet new guys. And maybe some of them won't be backstabbers or total jerks.

I take a deep breath, grab the handle of my suitcase, and set off to find a cab. The address of my new school, Saint Peter's Academy, is scribbled on a slip of paper, shoved deep into my coat pocket. *It'll be fine,* I tell myself as I hurry to one of the black cabs parked outside the airport.

Once I'm settled inside the stuffy warmth of the cab's backseat, I fish the paper out of my pocket and read it out loud to the driver. He huffs in exasperation when I finish, though I'm not sure why. The old man steps on the gas and the cab rockets forward, narrowly missing another cab parked along the sidewalk, waiting for a customer. The two drivers promptly flip each other off, yell out something about a wanker, whatever that is, and then we're out of the crowded parking lot.

The city of London whizzes by so quickly, I can barely make anything out through the wet and foggy windows. Shrugging out of my coat, I lay it across the seat to dry out and pull my cell phone from my purse. No new calls or texts. *Shocker.* Tossing it back into my bag, I lean my forehead against the cool window. My breath fogs the glass up quickly.

Absently, I find myself drawing stars in the condensation.

After a few minutes, the window looks like the sky at night, crowded with celestial beauty. I close my eyes and let the movement of the cab lull me into a sort of half-sleep, half-awake state. I can still hear the radio, the whoosh of the tires on the wet roads, but behind my closed eyelids, there's nothing but a sky full of brilliant stars.

The slam of a door wakes me, and I realize the cab is no longer moving and the driver isn't in his seat. Looking around, I see him meandering to the trunk, popping it open, and pulling my suitcase out. When I look out the window, I understand exactly why he huffed when I told him the address.

The cab is parked in front of a massive red brick building that looks to be at least a hundred years old, and hasn't been taken care of properly in at least half that long. The roof looks half-rotten and leaky, even from the street. The windows are caked with dirt and grime, and a few are even boarded up. The small grassy area out front clearly hasn't been tended to in a while; the weeds and grass are at least two feet tall. The flower beds under the large, rounded front windows are overrun by more weeds.

"This is it? Are you sure?" I ask as I slide out of the backseat and onto the cracked sidewalk. It doesn't look like much of a school, or like anyone lives here at all. How has my Uncle let the building get to this point?

The driver huffs again, depositing my suitcase onto the sidewalk. "You think I'd come all the way out here to this dump if I weren't sure?" he asks.

I look back at the sad, old building. *Maybe the inside isn't so bad,* I think. When I look back at the old man, his hand is out, palm up.

"Oh!" I say. "Sorry." I dig his payment out of the envelope

filled with the correct currency that Great Uncle Henry sent me, depositing it into the driver's upturned palm. Instantly, he turns, gets back in the cab, and drives away, leaving me standing in front of my new home.

I take a shaky breath, gather up my luggage, and start up the narrow sidewalk to the front door. I climb the stone steps slowly, taking in the age of the building. Something about it seems lovely to me. If it was restored, or at least properly cared for, it could be a magnificent place. At the top of the steps, I stop, staring at the tall oak door in front of me. Tentatively, I reach out and knock a few times. Nobody answers. I can't hear anything inside. No noise, no sign of anyone coming to the door, or of anyone being inside at all. I try the knob, which turns easily in my hand, and push open the door, stepping inside.

I was right—the inside of the building doesn't look quite as rundown as the exterior. But the smell… the smell is what hits me first. Damp, moldering wood, mixed with the sharp smell of cat pee. I gag and try to cover my nose with the collar of my coat. Looking around, I realize that the less than ideal interior doesn't stop at the smell. The railing on the formerly grand staircase is half falling off, while the stairs themselves look rickety and unable to hold even my modest weight. Everything is coated in a thick layer of dust, and the paint is literally peeling off the walls, exposing dated, ugly, floral wallpaper underneath.

Suddenly, I can't breathe, and not just because of the smell. The foyer seems to be closing in around me, suffocating me. *I can't do this.* Turning on my heel, I walk right back out the door without even glancing back. I hurry down the path to the sidewalk where I was deposited by the cab driver, gasping. My chest and throat feel tightly constricted. I sit down on top of my suitcase, gulping in the sweet, fresh air, not caring that the cold burns my lungs with each breath.

Once I've caught my breath and my heart has slowed to its normal pace, reality sinks in. I can't possibly stay here. But what else am I supposed to do?

"Alright, Elena," I say to myself. "Time to put on your big girl panties."

First things first: I need to find my Uncle Henry. My teeth are chattering, and now that the sun is going down, it's getting even colder. I'd really like to go inside and get warm. But the smell… I don't know if I can get past the smell. I can handle the building being old and rundown, but I'm not sure I can handle the smell. *At least it isn't raining anymore…*

Pulling my coat tighter around my body, I stand, gather my belongings, and stride purposefully back up the path to the door. I pull my collar over my nose in an attempt to block even some of the acrid smell. It doesn't work. My eyes water approximately ten seconds after entering the building. Blinking away the tears, I look around, trying to find my Great Uncle's office, or someone who can point me the right way.

There are doors on either side of the staircase, but both are closed. I let go of my suitcase handle and take a few steps forward. The heels of my black riding boots click loudly on the dark wood floors.

"Hello?" I call out, looking up toward the second floor. No answer. I turn, walking around the staircase. The building is bigger than I thought. A long hallway extends back behind the stairs. Closed doors line both sides of the hall. "Hello?" I call again, a little louder this time.

"In here, dear!" a male voice calls back. I peer around a corner that I didn't notice before to find an open door. Inside the small room, an elderly man is sitting behind a desk, looking down his long nose through a pair of spectacles at the paper in his hand. He looks up when I clear my throat. *Great Uncle Henry.*

"Ah, hello there. Elena, I presume?" he asks. I nod, a shy smile tugging at the corners of my mouth. Other than a few phone conversations and a handful of letters sent over the years to check in on me, I barely know this man.

"Good, good. I've been waiting for you," he smiles, standing. He retrieves a single key from a desk drawer and steps toward the door. "Follow me, dear. I'll show you to your room."

"I'm sorry. For the way I called you, for springing all of this on you," I say, hurrying to catch up with my uncle after grabbing my luggage.

"Elena, you are my niece," he replies, panting as he climbs the staircase. "I made it clear after your parents' untimely deaths that I would do whatever I could to help you."

My throat tightens. I barely know this man, my mother's uncle, and yet at the drop of a hat, he flew me here and is giving me a place to stay and to go to school. It's so nice of him. I don't know how I will ever repay him.

I test the first few steps with my toes before following him up. "Thank you," I say. I need to change the subject before I break down. "Where is everyone?" I ask, looking around at the huge, empty building.

"There are a few students around somewhere." Uncle Henry waves his hand. "But I'm afraid you will have the place mostly to yourself, as most of the students have gone home for the holiday."

I expected as much. Oh, well. I like being alone, and I'm sure my uncle will be here, and maybe I'll get to meet some of the kids still hanging around. The horrid smell that permeates the air of the foyer seems to fade a little the further away we get, thankfully. I suck in a deep breath of clean-ish air, running my hand over the smooth wood of the banister. It wiggles a little, threatening to fall off completely, so I snatch my hand back.

My uncle makes pleasant small talk as we walk, asking about my trip, if I need pocket money, if I have everything I need. I want to ask him about the smell, ask him why the building looks so uncared for, but I keep my thoughts to myself. He's an old man, and I'm sure he does what he can with the place.

Finally, we stop in front of an ordinary white door that looks like all the others lining the long hallway. He unlocks the door and looks down at me through the glasses still perched on his nose.

"This is your room, dear. You can clean it up and decorate it how you like, as long as you don't make any major changes to the structure," he tells me.

My mouth goes dry, so I just nod.

"I'll be taking off soon, but I'll be back tomorrow morning, so if you need anything…"

"I'm sure I can handle the night alone, Uncle Henry." I smile back at him. I want to tell him that I've had a lot of experience in taking care of myself—twelve years, to be exact—but something stops me. I can't bring myself to say the words.

The elderly man nods once and hands me the key to my room.

"In that case, I'll let you get settled," he smiles, then turns and walks away. Halfway back to the staircase, he turns and calls out, "Oh, and Elena? Don't try to open the windows. It's strictly forbidden."

I nod, wondering why opening windows would be forbidden, but I don't press him. Instead, I take a deep breath and open the door.

Two

The inside of the dorm room is quaint, but better than I expected from the look of the building's exterior and the smell of the foyer. The air in the dorm is stale, and everything is very plain, but after a little TLC, I think it will be perfectly livable. I drop my luggage on the floor of the small living room and walk through the door to the bedroom. I'm pleasantly surprised to see that I have a single. No backstabbing roommates this time.

The dorm room consists of two smaller rooms: a small living room and a small bedroom. In the bedroom is a large canopy bed that takes up most of the space. The canopy itself is dirty and moth-eaten, but once I replace it, it will be beautiful.

A faded old leather chair sits to one side of the bed, and on the other side is a small nightstand with a simple white lamp and a cheap digital alarm clock. There's a door that leads into my private—but tiny—bathroom. I have just enough space to walk around the bed to the window and get to the closet and the bathroom. Everything needs to be thoroughly cleaned, but other than a bit of dust, it will work just fine.

I stroll back into the living room, running my hands along the off-white walls. The few boxes containing my other belongings, which I sent over ahead of my arrival, are here, waiting for me on the faded red couch. I set them on the floor and sink down on the couch, a cloud of dust bursting from the fabric and puffing out all around me. I cough and stand, waving my hand to clear the air. Oh, well. I need a shower anyway.

As I rip open one of the boxes, the familiar smell of lavender and vanilla floats up to my nose. I press my nose into the cotton sheets and breathe deeply. The sheets smell like home. *No, this is home now*, I remind myself, carrying the box of linens into the bedroom. I pound on the mattress with my fist, releasing another large cloud of dust into the air. Coughing, I look at the tall window on the far wall. I know Uncle Henry said it was "strictly forbidden," but...

Screw it, I think, striding over and prying the window open. It squeals loudly, and I cringe, but no one comes running to tell me to shut it, and no alarm sounds, so I leave it open. The fresh air that floods into the room is like sweet relief. I wait for the dust to clear, then make the bed with my sheets. The lavender scent permeates the room, relaxing me. I yawn, realizing just how tired I really am after the long hours of travelling, then sniff the ends of my auburn hair. It smells like airplane. I wrinkle my nose and scrub at my face with my hands. My skin feels oily and grimy under my fingers. *Shower first, then sleep.*

I strip off the thick sweater that I've been wearing since I left Oregon, dropping it to the floor. Looking at the open window, I consider closing it—or at least pulling the thick red curtains closed—but decide against it. It's not like there's anyone to see me anyway. I turn away and cross the bedroom to the hot shower that awaits me, leaving a trail of discarded clothes as I go.

The hot water feels amazing on my skin. The room was chilly, and I forgot to turn the heat up before I got in, so I linger in the shower. It feels so good to scrub off the smell of airplane, taxi, and disgusting old building. I swear, the smell of the foyer soaked through my clothes and into my skin. Sticking my face directly into the water, I scrub as hard as I can with my hands, letting the water cascade over my head and down my body.

A sound in the other room catches my attention. A soft click, like the sound of the door closing or the window shutting. It's such a tiny sound that I immediately begin to think I imagined it; I locked the door, didn't I? And there's no way somebody got in through my second-story window. But I heard *something*; I know I did. Turning off the water, I grope around until I find the towel I laid out on the counter and wrap it tightly around myself.

I take a quick look around the tiny space. There's nothing that I can use as a weapon if there *is* someone in my room. The last thing I want to do is try to defend myself with no weapon, naked and soaking wet. But what else can I do? I take a deep breath and creep toward the open bathroom door. The bedroom is empty, and everything is still right where I left it, down to the discarded clothes on the floor. I creep through the bedroom and peek around the doorway into the living room. The door is still locked. No signs of entry.

I let out a sigh of relief. I knew it was just my mind playing tricks on me. Still, I cross the room to the window, close it, and draw the curtains shut before turning the heater on full blast and putting on leggings, an oversized long-sleeved shirt, and fuzzy socks. I brush my hair out and wrap it in the towel to dry. Outside, the world is quiet and still. A light snow is falling, blanketing the icy sidewalks and roads with pure white powder, undisturbed by footprints or tire tracks. It seems so peaceful. All the surrounding shops and buildings are dark, the only light coming from the few streetlamps along the road. Their yellow glow casts an eerie effect on the falling snow.

Clean and warm, I suddenly realize that I'm starving. I don't have to bother consulting the almighty internet to know that nothing is open, and even if it was, I wouldn't go out in the snow and the dark anyway. Rummaging through my luggage, I manage to find a bar of sea salted dark chocolate, a half empty bag of sunflower seeds, a bottle of diet soda, and a granola bar. They'll have to do. I eat my random assortment of snacks in silence, brush my teeth, and climb into bed.

I leave the lamp on, fear still pressing into my brain, and close my eyes, but sleep won't come. Lying there, the noise I thought I heard plays over and over again in my head. For some reason, even though I know it wasn't real, something about it has me spooked. Something about it is niggling at my brain, like the noise is refusing to be dismissed as imaginary. I toss and turn for what feels like hours, but every time I look at the flashing green numbers on the clock, only a few minutes have passed.

Random thoughts, images, and events pop into my mind. Some real, like the image of my ex-boyfriend and ex-best friend rolling on the floor together, some utterly ridiculous, like the vision of myself flying across a dark sky full of glittering stars, like in my dream during the cab ride this afternoon. My brain feels like it's going in a million directions at once. But eventually my eyes do close, and sleep does come—deep and dark and restless.

The boy with the strange green eyes waits until night has fallen to re-turn to the other world. The things people would say if they saw a boy flying over their precious city. But he is growing impatient; he does not want to wait any longer. He cannot seem to stay away from the beautiful girl. He wants her to know that he is coming for her, that he is going to take her away from that awful place. She will be happy in Neverland. No more tears, no more worries. He must give her a sign.

As soon as night falls in the other world, the boy goes to her. She has left her window open, practically inviting him inside. The boy risks a quick glance inside, only to find that the girl is not there. He drifts down until his feet touch the floor, and steps into the bright room. The boy can hear running water behind a closed door; she must be in there, bathing.

The boy's cheeks burn at the thought of her bare skin. He tiptoes through the room, forcing his thoughts in another direction. The room the girl inhabits here is depressing. Stark, bland, and positively boring. There are boxes piled against one wall, and the boy's curiosity gets the best of him. He crosses the floor quietly and begins poking through her belongings.

Everything in the boxes smells wonderful, like clean, sweet girl. The boy inhales her scent, basking in it, wanting nothing more than to bury his nose in her hair, breathe in the sweetness of her skin. The boy lifts a blanket from one of the flimsy boxes, needing more, but a small metal blade falls from the folds of fabric. He tries to catch it, but he is not quick enough. The metal hits the floor with a thud. The water in the other room stops.

As quickly and quietly as he can manage, the boy stuffs everything back into the boxes and disappears through the window.

When my eyes open again, the room is pitch black. I blink a

few times, my eyes slowly adjusting. It wasn't this dark when I laid down, was it? The green numbers on the alarm clock are flashing 1:13 A.M. They are the only light in the room. Sighing, I roll over in bed and switch on the lamp. An odd feeling comes over me when I do, like I've already done it before. I could have sworn the lamp was on when I laid down. I shake my head. No, I must have turned it off when I couldn't sleep. *Stupid jetlag.*

I get myself a drink of water from the bathroom, carrying it back to bed with me after checking the lock on the door once more. The curtains on the window are still closed. Still feeling exhausted, I lay back down, curling my body around one of the extra pillows I brought with me. Sleep comes much easier this time, and in minutes, I'm dreaming of flying through starry skies again.

⸻ ❈ ⸻

My eyes open to bright sunlight streaming in through the window. Rubbing my eyes, I prop myself up on my elbows and glance at the clock. The green numbers are flashing 1:07 P.M. I sigh. My schedule is completely screwed up.

I stumble into the bathroom to wash my face and brush my teeth, thinking all the while that maybe the move to London wasn't such a brilliant idea after all.

Returning to the bedroom, I drag my brush roughly through my auburn locks. That's when I realize what's different. The curtains are open. They were open when I woke up. But I swear that I closed the curtains before I went to bed. Yes, they were closed. I'm *sure* of it. My heartrate picks up. Someone *was* in here last night. The noise wasn't my imagination.

A cold sweat breaks out over my body. Who was in here? Where were they hiding that I couldn't see them in this tiny dorm room? Or did they re-enter after I fell asleep? None of the answers to those questions are good.

I zip around the room, taking quick stock of my belongings. My wallet and all of its contents are still here. So is the small amount of jewelry I own, not that any of it is very valuable. Nothing else I have in this room is valuable at all. Most of the boxes that contain my things aren't even open yet. A chill creeps over my skin, making me shudder.

I shake my head. I'm being ridiculous. *If* someone was in here, it was probably just Uncle Henry checking in on me before he left for the night. Or maybe it was one of the other students who stayed at school over the holiday. Yeah, that's it. There's a perfectly rational explanation.

With the intention of taking my mind off of possible intruders, I formulate a plan to make the most of the rest of my day. After sleeping half the day, I feel the urge to be productive.

I pull on a pair of jeans and a sweater before tugging on my boots and coat. Then, I consult the almighty internet on my phone to find the nearest place to buy cleaning supplies. With enough Clorox, Pledge, and elbow grease I can definitely turn the boring dorm into a place I actually want to live in. Maybe, just maybe, I can try to improve the rest of the building too. At the very least, I can try to get rid of the awful smell in the foyer.

The boy laughs at his clever jokes. When he saw how frightened the girl was, he knew that this was going to be such fun. He lounged on the roof, gazing up at the night sky, until the girl finally fell asleep. She shut her window, but made the mistake of not locking it. With his powers, the boy had no trouble getting the window open again.

He watches her for a long time as she sleeps, taking in her soft, delicate features: the slightly upturned nose, the full lips, and the fiery hair splayed across her pillow. She is more than he ever hoped to find. She is second only to his first love.

The boy shakes his head. He cannot let thoughts of her cloud his mind. He takes one final look at the beautiful girl sleeping deeply before him, turns out the light, and goes home.

I arrive back at the school, hands full of bags of cleaning tools and products. Slipping on a pair of yellow rubber gloves and a paper facemask, I rummage through the bags of groceries until I find the cans of air freshener I purchased. Slowly, I push the door open. The smell hits me in the face like a truck. Gagging behind the thin mask, I release a steady mist of lavender-scented air freshener. I circle the staircase, my finger never leaving the trigger of the bottle. By the time I make a full lap of the first floor, the can is empty. I tuck it under my arm and brandish the full one. Then I slowly make my way up the stairs, still constantly spraying. When I reach the top, I go right back down for the rest of my supplies.

Back at my room, I give the hallway one final spray of sweet-smelling mist before hauling all of my cleaning supplies inside. I make sure to lock the door behind me, just in case. Setting the can of air freshener down on the worn couch, I immediately get to work. Prying open all of the windows, I breathe deep. The fresh, cold air makes the space instantly better. It's such a stupid rule that nobody is allowed to open windows. The building, especially the first floor, would benefit greatly from a good airing out once in a while.

Later in the day, I plant my hands on my hips and nod once. *Job well done, Elena.* I grin.

I glance out the window, surprised to see the sun already setting. That's what sleeping half the day gets me, I guess. At least the rest of the day was productive. Heaving myself out of the leather chair, I haul all of the boxes, stuffed with the soiled linens from the dorm, and take them out into the hallway to be thrown out. By now, it's fully dark, and the snow has begun falling again. A shiver goes down my spine. What if whoever was in my room last night comes back?

Suck it up, buttercup! I chastise myself. I cannot lose it now, not when things are kind of starting to look up. I'll be fine. I'll just lock everything up tight, and I'll be *fine.* Everyone will be back from Christmas break in a little over a week, and then I can get into the swing of things. Until then, I practically have the whole school to myself.

My stomach growls viciously, and I realize that I haven't eaten anything all day, or really at all since I arrived in London. I grab my purse, make sure I have the money my uncle gave me, and look back at the dorm room. The shiny wood floors, the clean windows, the off-white walls.… It may not look like much right now, but I think I might actually like it here. I turn off the lights, lock the door and sprint down the stairs, holding my sweater over my nose to shield against the smell in the foyer.

On the first floor, I can see just a sliver of light peeking out from under Uncle Henry's office door. He will probably be the best person to ask for restaurant recommendations, mostly because he's the only person I've seen. I knock lightly on his door and watch as a shadow crosses the light spilling onto the floor. The door opens just a crack; all I can see is a spectacled eye.

"Sorry to bother you, Uncle Henry," I begin. "I was just wondering if you could point me in the direction of a decent restaurant."

"Elena, dear," he smiles, his eyes crinkling at the edges. "It's a shame you showed up over the holiday. The cooks here make wonderful food, they just aren't here now. But I'd be happy to escort you to dinner."

"I don't want to interrupt your work," I insist. "I've been cleaning my room all afternoon and I'm kind of dirty. I just thought I'd get some take-out and finish what I started."

Uncle Henry nods, but he does look a little disappointed that I didn't accept his dinner invitation. I promise him that we will reschedule our dinner for another night, when I've had a chance to clean up, and that seems to appease him. He spends the next few minutes listing off restaurant and street names that I've never heard before.

When my uncle finishes giving me detailed directions to each place he named, despite my insistence that I could just use my phone to find them, I say my goodbye and my thank you and head out the door. I try to remember as many as I can to punch into the GPS on my phone. Without it, I have a feeling I would get lost in about twenty seconds, and the last thing that I want is to get lost in an unfamiliar city, at night, while it's snowing.

Hustling down the sidewalk, I skirt icy spots and do my best to keep my balance. But before I get too far away, I turn back to look at the building. I can see dim light in one of the second-floor windows, shining behind a set of semi-sheer curtains.

While I stand watching, my coat pulled tight around my body, shielding me from the snow falling heavily from the gunmetal grey sky, one of the curtains pulls back just a tiny bit. I can see the silhouette of a head peek around the curtain and lift my hand to wave, but just as I do, the curtain falls shut again.

THREE

With a bag full of food in hand, I run down the road as fast as I can without slipping on the ice and snow. One of the names Uncle Henry gave me happened to be the name of a little café just a few blocks from the school. The inside of the restaurant smelled amazing. It made my mouth water instantly, and I didn't hesitate to order everything that sounded good. The smell of my dinner wafting up out of the bags makes my stomach rumble and my feet move a little faster.

As much as I don't want to admit it, I'm kind of glad to be going back to my new school. I have a feeling that once I put my personal touch on my dorm room, it will feel like home. Hell, I might even be happy here. I take one corner a little too fast and slip on a patch of ice, landing flat on my back. The air rushes out of my lungs all at once with a hiss. "Ouch," I mumble, pushing myself to my feet. The back of my jeans and coat are wet from the snow. Miraculously, none of my food spilled onto the wet sidewalk. My teeth chatter and I shiver the rest of the way back.

Less than ten minutes later, I'm back in my dorm, spreading out the ridiculous amount of food I ordered: a big turkey sandwich, a cup of soup, a large grilled chicken salad, and even a piece of chocolate cake for dessert. It looks and smells wonderful. At this point I'm ravenous, my stomach twisting with hunger. I take a large bite of the sandwich and sip a little of the steaming soup, feeling instantly better.

It doesn't take me long to wolf it all down, including the cake. Afterward I feel satiated—revived, almost. Looking around the living room, I feel like I should probably finish unpacking and putting my stuff away. The little living room is littered with everything I own. My books are piled next to the door; my framed art prints and pictures are strewn across the floor near the far wall. But instead, I shower quickly, change into a pair of black leggings, a tank top, and my favorite cardigan, wrap myself in my favorite chunky knit blanket, and lay down on the bed.

The smell of lavender laundry soap and vanilla relax me instantly. Warm and with a full stomach, I drift off. This time, though, my dreams aren't happy. This time there's no sky full of brilliant stars, no calm sea, and no weightless, happy feeling. This time, dark figures emerge from the shadows, reaching for me. I run down the street, unsure if I'm running away from something or toward something. The streetlights cast an eerie yellow glow on the scene, and under the one closest to me, the dark shape of a man leans against the post. As I get closer, he lifts his head, and in the middle of a face made of shadow is a pair of the strangest green eyes I've ever seen.

My eyes open to dim grey light filtering in through the window, then close again, still heavy with sleep. But something makes them fly open again. The curtains are open. *Again.* Whipping back the covers, I launch myself out of bed, close the curtains, and look wildly around. *What the hell is going on?* I think, panic rising in my chest. The room is freezing. It's so cold that I can see my breath puffing out in little white clouds in front of my face. Those curtains were shut, and the heater was on. I knew it. I'm *not* crazy. I've always had this weird thing about needing to close the curtains or blinds before I go to sleep. Something about it just makes me feel safer. And after the last couple nights, it feels even more necessary, so I'm almost positive that I closed them.

I repeat the words over and over in my head while I dig through my closet for a cardigan. *I am not crazy. I am not crazy. I am NOT crazy.* I pull the cardigan on over my thin tank top, slip my feet into my Ugg boots, and drape a scarf around my neck. Quickly, I make a lap of the rooms. Nothing is missing. I shake my head and repeat *I am not crazy* once more. My heart starts to slow the longer I tell myself that I forgot to close the curtains, that I forgot to turn the heater up.

I locate my little coffee maker, plug it in, and load it with a filter and some of my favorite coffee that I brought from the States. I don't have milk or sugar, so I can't make it as well as I usually do, but any caffeine is better than none. Sipping the hot black coffee, I carefully place my pictures on the nightstand next to the bed and side table in the living room. Then I turn to my book collection, loading them all onto the bookshelf, wondering the whole time if the sad little thing is going to collapse under their weight.

After finishing my second cup of coffee, I look around. I make a mental note to buy a new canopy for the bed tomorrow.

It's coming together nicely, but still needs a *lot* of work. It would be amazing if I could paint the walls. A light, smoky grey would be ideal to go with my color palate. But I highly doubt my uncle will let me do that.

I wander through the apartment for most of the morning, finding random places to put my few possessions. I even find some sticky strips to hang my framed prints and posters on the wall. By lunchtime, I don't have anything left to do, but the dorm looks much more like, well, *me*. I pick a book from my small personal library and try reading for a while, but I get bored quickly and decide to explore the school instead. What better time to do so than when it's empty?

In his little wooden house up in the trees, the boy contemplates how he can convince the girl to come with him. He doesn't doubt his charm or his abilities, but this girl is different. She isn't as susceptible to pretty words and promises as other girls are. He's seen enough of her lonely life to know that much. Plus, she was suspicious after his little stunts with the curtains. He thought his jokes were quite funny, but she did not seem amused.

The boy can easily convince her to come along; all he has to do is look into her eyes and she will bend to his will. But where is the fun in that? Perhaps if he sends a fairy to retrieve her… yes, that could work. Girls love fairies, and if another female comes to her first, she might be more willing to listen, to accept his offer. The boy smiles at his own cleverness. He summons the fairy.

FOUR

I wander aimlessly through the deserted, dilapidated old building, half of me hoping that I'll run into one of the other students, the other half perfectly content roaming the halls alone. Trailing my fingers along the banister of what was once the grand staircase, I wonder who was peeking out from behind that curtain last night. Whoever it was didn't seem all that friendly. Or maybe they're just shy.

Strolling along the landing, I peer down at the first floor, wondering if my uncle is still around. The door to his office is closed, though, so probably not. Not that I want to bother him, but he's the only person I know right now, even if I don't know him well.

The sharp, sour smell that seems to constantly linger in the front half of the building reaches my nose. I wrinkle it and turn away, walking toward the other side of the building.

Peering around the corner, I see that it is identical to the one my room is in. I decide to take a look anyway. Some of the doors have little windows in them, so I stretch up on my tiptoes to look inside. The first room is a small classroom. Three rows of old-fashioned desks with the chairs attached are lined up in front of a large wooden desk with a greenish blackboard hanging on the wall behind it. *Boring,* I think, moving on to the next, which is a science lab. Tall tables are scattered about the room with stools surrounding them. On the tables sit an assortment of beakers, test tubes, and Bunsen burners. On the teacher's desk, something floating in a large jar of cloudy yellow liquid catches my attention. I squint, trying to make out what it is, only to realize that it is a fetal pig. *Boring and gross.*

I sigh. The rest of the rooms with windows are just more classrooms. The doors with no windows are either more dorm rooms or maybe offices. I don't really care. I walk the full length of the long hallway, only to find that it's a dead end. Turning on my heel, I meander back towards the front of the building. I've been exploring for over an hour now, and I still haven't seen another soul. It's a little eerie, if I'm being honest.

Suddenly, I hear a door close in the other hall. I quicken my pace to a jog, hurrying to catch them before they exit the building. Just as I reach the landing, a boy with longish blond hair is just starting down the stairs.

"Hey!" I call out, panting. *Man, I'm out of shape.*

The boy spins around to face me, his eyes wide with surprise.

"Oh," he says. "Hi." But that's all he says before trying to escape again.

"Wait," I call again. But he just keeps going. I roll my eyes and follow him, taking the stairs two at a time until I'm right behind him. "Are you really just going to ignore me?" I ask. The boy's shoulders rise and fall as he sighs, then turns back to me.

"Sorry, I'm just going to grab some lunch down the street," he shrugs.

"So that means you can't talk to me for like, two minutes?" I demand, crossing my arms. "You're the first person I've seen since I got here. Well, aside from my uncle."

The boy rolls his eyes and smiles up at me from a couple stairs below. "So, you're the new girl?" he asks, looking me up and down.

When his eyes meet mine again, I see that they're brown, but not just plain old brown. Deep, dark brown, like melted chocolate. When he smiles again, I notice the chip in one of his front teeth. *He's cute.*

"That's me," I reply, leaning against the banister. It shifts under my weight, and I straighten instantly, my eyes going wide. The boy laughs. I pretend not to notice. "I'm Elena," I say, twining my fingers together.

"Cash," he replies. "Nice to meet you."

I flash him a smile. A few long moments pass where neither of us says anything. "So, umm, you were saying something about lunch?" I ask, batting my eyelashes at him. He's nice, and cute, and I could do way worse for a lunch date.

"Oh," he says, scratching the back of his head. "Yeah. I'd invite you along, but I'm kind of meeting my mom…" he trails off.

Awkward. "Oh, yeah, sure, no problem," I say, shifting my weight from one foot to the other. My cheeks are burning with embarrassment. "I'll just see you around or something," I mumble, turning and bounding back up the stairs without looking back, even when Cash calls out "Elena, wait!" That's what I get for trying to make a friend…

After eating lunch from the café a few blocks away, *alone*, I find myself officially and thoroughly bored. I try reading again, something I've always enjoyed. It's easy to get lost in fictional worlds when the real world is so crappy. But I can't even get into my book today. With nothing else to do, I decide that my best option is a nap. Curling up under my familiar sheets, in the unfamiliar room, in an unfamiliar building and city, I drift off. In my dreams, I visit somewhere that seems familiar, though I don't know why.

The room is dark when I wake. My eyes adjust quickly, and I glance around. Goosebumps erupt on my skin. *Something isn't right.* I can feel it. A change in the air—it feels charged, like it does right before a lightning storm. But what could it be? Then I see her. There's a girl sitting in the worn leather armchair opposite the bed, staring at me in the darkness.

A strangled, piercing scream that I didn't know I was capable of producing fills the room. I scramble out of the bed, feeling around for something—anything—that I can use as a weapon. Without taking my eyes off the girl, I stick my hand into the drawer of the nightstand by the bed. It's mostly empty; I feel pens and my stationary, a box of envelopes, paperclips…. Then my hand touches something cold, something metal. I pull an old-fashioned letter opener out, one of the ones with a carved handle and sharp metal blade. It'll have to do.

Brandishing the letter opener like a knife, I straighten up, pointing it at the girl. She hasn't moved at all. She's still just sitting in the chair on the other side of the bed, legs crossed underneath her, watching me with an almost amused look on her face. "Who are you?" I ask, my voice loud but shaky. "What do you want?"

The girl puts her hand to her mouth and giggles. It's high-pitched, like a child's laugh. But she can't be a child; kids younger than high school age don't go to this school. How did she get in? "Who are you?" I ask again. The letter opener in my hand is shaking along with my voice. The girl stands, and when she does, I second-guess my assumption that she isn't a child.

She's quite small, maybe five feet tall. Her hair is so blonde it's almost white. It practically glows in the dark, and is styled in a messy bun piled on top of her head. The coil of hair is held in place by what looks like a clip in the shape of a large leaf. She's wearing a long, moss green tunic and leggings the color of wet earth. On her feet is a pair of soft-looking slippers the color of her tunic, with more leaves adorning them.

The girl giggles again. "I'm a fairy, of course!"

Now I'm the one laughing. A *fairy*! It's one of the most absurd things I've ever heard. I lower the blade in my hand. This girl is clearly just a little girl who wandered away from home and ended up here somehow. "Where are your parents?" I ask the girl, my voice much gentler now. "Do you go to this school?"

She giggles again. "Of course not," she says, her voice like a silver bell. "I'm from Neverland!"

I laugh harder. But then something clicks in my head. I locked the door when I got home from the café, and never unlocked it again. Right? Slowly, I reach out and switch on the lamp by the bed. With the letter opener still in my hand, I walk slowly backwards to the door. Peeking out into the living room, I see that the door is still locked. All of the windows in my dorm room are closed. So how did this girl get inside my second story room?

When I look at her again, I notice that she doesn't look as childlike in the light. She's still very small, but her facial features are almost foreign-looking, sharp and angular, not soft like a child's. Her deep green eyes are glittering with excitement, or maybe it's mischief; I can't tell. What I thought was a clip in her hair appears to be a real leaf, and the ones on her shoes look real too. "H-How did you get in here?" I stammer.

The girl—I can't bring myself to call her a fairy—lets out another high-pitched giggle. "Magic, silly!" she exclaims.

My mouth drops open. This is ridiculous. This can't be happening right now. I poke myself in the finger with the tip of the letter opener. *Nope, definitely not dreaming.* "Listen," I begin, wiping the droplet of blood on my pants. "I don't know who you are, or why you're here, or how you got in. But if you leave now, we can just forget this ever happened."

A confused look flits across the girl's face. She puts her hands on her hips and scowls at me. "I already told you. I'm a fairy! My name is Tatiana. I got in using magic. As for why I'm here… to see you!" She finishes by sticking her lower lip out in a distinctly childish pout that contradicts her glittering green glare.

I'm starting to lose my temper now. I can feel it simmering beneath the surface of my skin, rising in my chest. "Fine, *Tatiana*," I spit. "You want me to believe that you are who say you are, that you have magic? Well then, prove it!"

Her pout disappears, replaced by a triumphant smile. "Easy!" she trills. "Watch this!" She snaps her fingers and vanishes into thin air.

I blink dumbly, frozen in place. "What just happened?" I murmur. Then I hear the giggle coming from behind me. I spin around to find a glowing ball of light hovering eye-level in the air. I blink again and squint, trying to look closer.

Inside the ball of light is the girl. Somehow, she's shrunken herself—she's no more than a couple inches tall now. A pair of iridescent wings have sprouted from her back and are fluttering quickly, like a hummingbird. She lifts a tiny hand and waves before flying over my head, giggling the whole time. When I turn around, she's normal-sized again, but she's perched on the metal bars meant to hold the canopy over the bed.

"How did you do that?" I ask, the awe audible in my voice.

"I told you, magic!" she says, smiling smugly.

"Magic," I repeat. "Magic is… *real*?"

"Of course magic is real!" she giggles, swinging her feet.

Magic is real… *no*. It can't be. Can it? Fairies aren't real. Neverland isn't real. Magic isn't real. But, how else can I explain what I just saw? Unless I'm losing my mind.

"You said you're here to see me? *Why?*" I ask, sinking down to the floor.

"Oh, yes!" she exclaims. Gracefully, she flips backward off the metal bar, landing on her feet in the leather chair. She sinks down into the cross-legged position she was in when I first saw her. "I've come to take you back with me!" she says with a little clap.

"Back? Back where?" I ask, even though I'm fairly certain I already know what she's going to say.

"Why, to Neverland, of course!" she smiles brightly.

"Neverland…" I breathe.

Everyone has heard of Neverland. It's the magical world made famous by many different books and movies, starting with the classic story written by J.M. Barrie. Neverland is home to fairies, mermaids, pirates like the infamous Captain Hook, and Peter Pan. But those are just stories. Not real. Unless… it is real. Maybe it's always been real.

Maybe Barrie visited the magical world once, and that's what inspired his most famous story. What if we have just been conditioned to not believe, all because most people don't have enough imagination to believe that somewhere like that can truly exist?

Or maybe I've just finally gone completely insane, and this is all an elaborate hallucination.

"So, you're Tatiana, a fairy. And you're here to take me to Neverland. Do I have that right?" I ask. Tatiana nods emphatically. "Right. So, um, why did you come for *me?*"

Tatiana giggles. "He sent me. He has been watching you since you arrived in London, before that even. He wants to meet you."

"Peter Pan wants to meet me? But why?" I ask, choosing not to add in a question about why the hell Peter Pan has been watching me for who knows how long. Tatiana narrows her eyes, like she's getting annoyed by all of my questions. What did she expect? That she'd show up and I'd just go off with her, no questions asked? Not likely. "Well?" I prompt her, crossing my arms over my chest.

"Peter Pan; that's a silly name!" she laughs. Because sure, that's what's strange about this whole thing…

"His name is Aiden. He is the ruler of Neverland, and he has been searching for just the right girl for a very long time," she says.

For the first time, I notice her odd accent. It's not British, or French, or German. It's lilting and melodic, despite her high-pitched voice. But I can't place it.

"Why is he looking for the perfect girl? The perfect girl for *what*?" I demand. I don't care if she's annoyed. I'm not going anywhere until I get some answers. Even then, I still might not go.

"To be his queen, of course! And to be the mother to all of the lost children on Neverland!" The fairy spreads her arms wide as she talks.

"This Aiden, ruler of Neverland, wants me to be his *queen*? Queen of Neverland? And a *mother* to the lost boys?" I ask. I'm aware that I'm pretty much just repeating everything she says in the form of a question, but I just can't seem to wrap my head around this whole thing.

Tatiana sighs. "Yes! Now come! We must go before dawn breaks!" She jumps out of the chair and starts opening one of the bedroom windows.

"Wait!" I cry. "I can't just go. I have responsibilities, like school and… and I have more questions!"

"Enough questions!" The fairy snaps, clenching her tiny fists at her side. "We must go now! Aiden can answer your inane questions when we get to Neverland."

I shrink back against the wall, sliding down to the floor,

not expecting such an angry answer from the little fairy girl. It scares me a bit that she can snap that easily, especially now that I've seen some of her magic. "No!" I say as firmly as I can. "I'm not going anywhere with you. If he wants me, he can come and get me himself!"

Tatiana turns, her green eyes practically glowing with anger. She starts coming toward me, her hands balled into little fists. I hold the letter opener up in an attempt to hold her off. I may be bigger than she is, but my little blade is no match for magic. She stops, her face turning red. I can feel my body trembling with fear and anger, but I'm determined not to let her see it.

Tatiana takes a couple more steps toward me; then there's a bright flash of light and she's tiny again, just a glowing ball of light. In the blink of an eye, she flies out the window, and I'm left alone in my bedroom again.

I blink a few times, trying to make sense of everything that just happened. I met a *fairy,* and not just *any* fairy, a fairy from *Neverland.* And she was kind of… mean, when she didn't get her way. I found out that magic is real, that Neverland is real. Are other magical worlds from the stories real too? The Enchanted Forest, Narnia, Middle Earth—are those places real too? Is there a war going on in space that we don't know about, like in Star Wars? The possibility that those places could truly exist makes my head hurt.

Pushing myself off the floor, I hurry to the window and slam it closed, flipping the latch at the top to lock it. Then I go through and lock all the other windows, and I check the lock on the door again too. I doubt that Tatiana will be back tonight, or that locks would stop her, but just in case. The sky outside is still dark, the world outside lost in their dreams. Not me, though. I don't think I'll be able to close my eyes after the encounter with Tatiana.

I put on a pot of coffee and grab my copy of *Peter Pan* off the bookshelf. Settling onto the ugly red couch, I run my fingers over the front cover. I've read this book at least ten times, but it never gets old. It was my favorite fairy tale as a kid. It was the first book I learned to read on my own. My mind reels at the thought that it could all be true. I take a sip from the steaming mug of black coffee and open to page one. Within minutes, I'm completely immersed in the book.

I only stop reading long enough to refill my mug with coffee. By the time I'm done, the sun is high in the sky. All the plans I had for the day are shot, but I'm content. *Peter Pan* is such a beautiful story, but something about it bothers me. In the story, Peter Pan is a young boy. But I am not a little girl. I'm a seventeen-year-old girl. Practically a woman! What would a pre-teen boy want with a queen, especially one much older than him? Why wouldn't he find someone his own age, like Wendy from the story? It doesn't make sense.

Shaking my head, I stretch my stiff limbs and rise from the couch. My stomach growls, but I barely notice. My head is full of fantasies of flying off to Neverland to meet the fairies and the mermaids. I place the book back on the shelf and wander into the bedroom. I can't get the fantastic thoughts out of my head. What if only some of the story is true? What if the place and the people are real, but other aspects of the story aren't?

I sit down on the bed, move to the chair, back to the bed, then stand again. I can't stay still, and my brain won't stop going at lightning speed. My stomach growls again, louder this time. Slipping on my boots and coat, I decide that a walk in the fresh air and some food will probably help me more than anything right now.

⸻❖⸻

Back in the treehouse, the boy with the strange green eyes glowers at the tiny blonde fairy. "What do you mean she would not come?" he growls at her.

The fairy, hovering in mid-air, shrinks back against the wooden wall. "I am sorry!" she squeaks. "I tried to tell her, to convince her like you told me! But she asked so many questions. And when she refused to come, I did not know what else to do!"

The boy glares at her, his eyes narrowed into slits. "I suppose that's what I get for sending a fairy to do a boy's work," he murmurs, standing. "You're dismissed." He waves his hand at the fairy.

She doesn't waste any time disappearing through the door. If the girl wouldn't listen to the fairy, he'd just have to go and retrieve her himself. The boy smiles, his green eyes shining with mischief and steps through the door. He closes his eyes and flies into the dark.

FIVE

After consulting the list of restaurants that my uncle gave me, I choose one at random and set off down the hallway, down the stairs, and out into the late afternoon. The walk there is full of more fantasies, but the walk back is full of thoughts of the food I can smell in the bag I'm carrying. Skirting the growing number of icy patches on the sidewalk, I hurry back to the school, eager to eat.

When I push the door to the building open, Cash is there in the foyer.

"Hello, Elena," he smiles. "How are you today?"

"I'm alright." I smile back. He looks me over, his eyes bouncing back up to my face after landing on the bag of food in my hand.

"I could have sworn I heard a scream somewhere in the building late last night. Did you hear it?" he asks, cocking his head to the side.

The scream he heard was me when I discovered Tatiana in my bedroom. But I can't tell him that. He would never believe me.

"No, I didn't. I wonder who it could have been," I reply, looking down at my boots.

"Hmm…" he says, a concerned look on his face. "Weird."

I nod, still not able to meet his eyes. "Well, I'm just heading back to my room to eat," I say quickly, holding up the bag of food. "Hope everyone is okay."

Cash smiles again, but it doesn't reach his eyes this time. I give him a small wave before hurrying up the stairs, guilt weighing on my heart from lying to him. But I couldn't tell him. He'd never understand. Nobody would understand, much less believe me. I lock the door behind me and settle on the couch to eat.

❦

When I'm done, my head feels a little clearer. The fantasies have stopped, replaced by an endless string of questions. Too bad there's no one to answer them. I decide to take a long, hot shower, hoping it will clear my head further and wash away some of the questions rolling through my mind. When I step out of the bathroom in my fuzzy pink robe, a towel wrapped around my head, I feel a little better. Until I realize that someone is once again sitting in the leather chair by my bed.

But this time, it isn't Tatiana. This time, it's a boy. A beautiful boy who looks to be my age, or close to it. His hair is sandy brown, but with streaks of light blond that shine like gold when he turns his head to look at me. The untidy waves hang down

into his eyes. Oh, those eyes. They are both beautiful and unnerving, so bright green they're almost neon. His striking gaze
lands on me, and when we lock eyes, my skin goes hot and cold
all at once. Something about them seems so familiar, but I know
I've never seen him before. I'd remember someone who looked
like him.

I force myself to look away, only to realize that now I'm
looking at his half-naked body. His lean, muscular chest is bare,
the skin a deep golden color. All he has on is a pair of moss
green pants, patched here and there with brown squares. Atop
his golden-brown head is a crown. Simple, rudimentary even.
Translucent green stones held in place by a circle of gold. They
don't really even look like stones, actually. More like pieces of
glass, and they are almost exactly the color of his eyes.

"Hello," he says. His incredible green eyes travel down my
body, taking in my towel-wrapped hair and fuzzy robe. The corners of his mouth twitch up in a small, amused smile.

"Um, hello," I reply, clutching the robe to my chest. "Are
you...?"

"Aiden," he says, standing. He folds one arm over his torso,
the other across his back, and bows to me. When he straightens,
he's smiling a full smile, revealing teeth that are slightly crooked on the bottom. The only imperfection I've noticed about him
so far. "You must be Elena. It's nice to finally meet you."

He offers me his hand. I don't take it. "I thought you were
supposed to be a little boy," I blurt out, my cheeks flaming in
response.

He laughs. "I'm no more grown-up than you, darling." His
voice is deep and melodic, and he speaks with the same odd,
lilting accent as Tatiana. "I am but a boy of seventeen," he continues.

So, he is my age, I find myself thinking as I look at him. He's
stunningly attractive.

"I'm sorry, I didn't mean to be rude," I say, my cheeks still hot. He starts to come toward me, and despite my obvious attraction to him, I find myself stepping back.

"No need to fear me," he says, holding his hands up. "I mean you no harm. I only wish you to be my queen."

I snort in response. I can't help it. "Why would you want me to be your queen? You don't know me," I say. His lips twitch up again.

"Oh, but I do know you. I've been watching you for a very long time, Elena."

A shiver runs down my spine. "How long *have* you been watching me, exactly?" I ask, inching back even farther until my back presses against the wall.

"I have visited you often over the past few years. I was very pleased when you came to London," Aiden says, still coming toward me.

I don't have anywhere to go now, and my heart rate begins to speed up. "You were in my room; you're the one who opened my curtains," I say quietly. He nods once. I wipe my sweaty palms on my robe. "You didn't answer my first question. Why me?" I ask, hoping he can't hear the fear in my voice.

"Because you are as I am. Alone in the world, and beautiful," he answers.

Biting my lip, I look him over again. He's beautiful, of course, and he seems harmless enough. But something about the way he's looking at me prevents me from relaxing completely. I say the only thing I can think of that might deter him. "You know I'm probably older than you, right?"

Aiden merely smiles. "Age is just a number, Elena. In Neverland, age is nothing. You will stay as you are. Young and beautiful, forever."

"Isn't the boy from Neverland supposed to be in love with Wendy?" I ask, thinking of the story. When I say the name Wendy, his eyes go dark for just a split second, like a cloud passing across the sun. It's gone so fast, replaced by a dazzling smile, that I wonder if I even saw it at all.

"You must be speaking of the storybook. You mustn't believe everything in your stories, darling," he says, looking at his filthy nails.

I don't know how to respond, so I take the towel off my hair and skirt around him, laying it down on the bed. When I turn back to face him, he's already there, his face just inches from mine.

"Come with me, Elena," he murmurs. He sidesteps around me until I can feel his warm breath on my neck. "Come with me to Neverland, where you will never grow old. We can have grand adventures and bathe in the Never Sea; we can watch the fairies dance in the moonlight and be together, forever," he whispers.

He's so close that I can smell him. He smells of trees and earth, and something else… something sweet and spicy all at once. I turn to face him, immediately entranced by his eyes.

"Come with me," he whispers.

I can't form a coherent thought, much less a sentence. But of its own accord, somehow, my head is nodding. A smile spreads wide across Aiden's face. He takes a few steps backward, leading me toward the bedroom window. Then he turns to go out, and when his eyes leave mine, my trance is broken.

"Wait!" I cry. "If I'm going to go off with you to Neverland, I need to bring some things with me." I look down at the fuzzy pink robe. "At the very least, I need to put some clothes on." When he turns back to face me, I see anger in his eyes, in the tightness of his mouth. But it dissipates quickly, replaced by a sweet-as-honey smile.

"Of course," he says through clenched teeth. "Do what you must."

I turn away, fear coursing through my veins. I shouldn't be doing this. Something screams, *WRONG!*

I grab some clothes out of my closet and lock myself in the

bathroom. Placing my hands on the edge of the sink, I take a long look in the mirror. My auburn hair hangs in wet waves, framing my face. My hazel eyes are wide with a mix of fear and excitement.

Am I really going to do this? Am I really going to drop everything and go off to Neverland with this guy? It's not like I'm leaving much behind. If Neverland is as wonderful as I'm thinking it will be, I won't even miss this world. But then Uncle Henry's kind old face, and Cash's handsome one, flash through my mind. My uncle will wonder what happened to me; he'll worry about me if I'm just gone one day.

A little voice inside of me whispers, *who cares if they worry, who cares if they report you as a runaway or a missing person, you'll be in Neverland dancing with fairies and swimming with mermaids, you don't need them.* As the words roll through my mind, the confusion and fear fade away. A childish grin spreads across my face.

I'm going to Neverland.

Quickly, I pull on the leggings, long white tunic, and olive-green cardigan I got from the closet. I unlock the door and pull it open to find Aiden lounging on my bed, legs crossed at the ankles, hands behind his head. My mouth drops open at the sight of him. Aiden grins in response, like he knows exactly how stunning he looks, exactly what effect he has on me. Forcing myself to turn away, I set about my task.

First, I find a decent-sized tote bag in the closet. Then I start stuffing as much as I can into it. A few changes of clothes, my favorite blanket that still smells like my laundry detergent, a few small items that have some semblance of value to me. I scan the room, looking for anything else I may need for a trip to Neverland. My eyes land on the bookshelf in the living room. I cross the space in a few steps, grab my copy of *Peter Pan,* and shove it to the bottom of the bag.

When I get back to the bedroom, Aiden looks up at me expectantly. I nod once, too nervous to smile or speak. In the blink of an eye, he's standing dangerously close to me again. "Close your eyes," he says quietly. I obey. A cool mist blows across my face. When my eyes open, I'm hovering a foot off the bedroom floor. A glittery green haze is surrounding me. *Fairy dust*, I think, smiling. When Aiden brushes his hands together, more green powder falls from his palms. "Fairy dust." He winks, as if he could read my mind.

I'm drifting higher, unable to control my own gravity. My head brushes the ceiling, making me giggle like a little girl. Then Aiden is there, guiding me toward the open window. I shoulder my bag and squeeze through the window, out into the cold winter night. Immediately, I wish I had dressed warmer, but the thought is pushed aside quickly. Stretched out before me—*no, underneath me*—is the grand city of London.

Aiden takes my hand and flies me higher until the whole city of London is laid out, nothing but a dense web of glittering lights. I gasp, the sudden intake of cold air burning my lungs. It's absolutely beautiful.

"I'm flying!" I say excitedly, spinning in the air to take in the sights.

Aiden's hand is warm in mine, and when I look at him, his strange green eyes are bright in the dark night, brighter than I thought possible. He's looking at me with amusement and wonder, a smile playing on the edges of his lips. "Come, darling. Dawn will be breaking soon," he says, tugging me along.

Aiden flies me over the sleeping city below, past Buckingham Palace, past Big Ben, over the London Bridge, and up, up to dizzying heights. The city below grows smaller and smaller, until the lights wink out of existence.

"Where is Neverland? How do we get there?" I call to Aiden over the roar of the wind rushing by. He points to a spot in the distance, to a bright cluster of stars in the black sky. "Second star to the right, and straight on 'til morning!" he calls over his shoulder. *At least I know one part of the story is true*, I grin to my-self.

Behind us, the sky is beginning to lighten at the edge of the horizon. Dawn. Suddenly, we're flying faster. The wind whips my hair around my face, threatening to tear my bag from my shoulder. I hold it tight against my side, afraid to lose the only things I'll have to remember my life in this world. The higher we go, the colder it gets. My feet feel like blocks of ice, and only now do I realize that I didn't put on any shoes. But still we go higher, closer to the stars that once were just flickering dots in the sky, but now are huge and blazing.

We're so close to the particular star that Aiden pointed out that I can feel its heat now. It thaws my numb body.

But then fear sets in.

Fear that if we don't stop, we will get too close and burst into flame ourselves. The heat gets even more intense; instead of shivering, I'm sweating now. My heart is hammering in my chest. "Aiden!" I call out. He doesn't respond, doesn't look at me, just gives my hand a tight squeeze and flies on.

Then there's a flash of pure white light, and somehow, we are flying faster. We're surrounded by stars, but flying so fast that they blur into streaks of multicolored light around us. Up ahead, the sky is lightening. But how is that possible, when just a moment ago the sun was behind us?

The night around us turns from dark blue to light, then to orange, then pink. Another flash of white. We slow instantly, now flying lazily over a deep blue body of water. I can smell salt and wind. It must be an ocean. I look up at a brilliant blue sky and know instantly that we've arrived. I'm in Neverland.

Six

Aiden lets go of my hand and turns onto his back, dropping lower and lower until his outstretched hands skim the water below. I'm flying by myself now—really flying! All because of magic. All those years as a child that I spent playing at magic, at fairytales, when all along they were real. Tightening my grip on my bag, I fly closer to the ocean. I reach down, letting my fingertips skim the surface.

A giggle erupts from my mouth. I don't remember ever feeling this happy. Aiden laughs too and flies higher. I follow, taking in the endless ocean around me. A minute later, a large ship comes into view. No, not just a ship, a *pirate* ship. The blood red sails and black flag are enough to convince me of that. I fly closer to Aiden. "Is that…" I start to ask.

"The *Jolly Roger*. Yes," Aiden says, his face suddenly hard.

As the ship grows closer, I can see men on the deck. Some are adjusting the sails, others coiling rope or tossing buckets of what I hope is water over the side. They all turn their heads to watch us fly past. I wave at them, laughing, and dip lower. At the wheel, one man pulls a long brass telescope out of his black coat, pointing it in our direction. I wave to him too as I zoom by, my arms stretched wide and a smile on my face.

"This way!" Aiden calls, veering away from the ship and pointing to a spot in the distance.

I follow, eager to see more of this world he's brought me to. The spot grows larger, revealing itself as a large island. A little way off the coast, a smaller island rises from the ocean, shrouded in mist and darkness. It looks menacing and evil, even from the air. A shudder ripples through me. Not wanting to spoil my first wonderful minutes in Neverland, I turn my attention back to the bigger island.

The large mass of land is bathed in golden sunlight, giving it an almost ethereal glow. Most of it is covered in dense jungle. A sea of green in the middle of the blue sea. A flock of bright orange birds rises into the air from the foliage. Aiden begins to make a wide circle around the island, allowing me to glimpse a large, rocky cove at one end. The rest of the shores are made of white, sandy beaches, like something you'd see on a postcard.

A group of long wooden boats are lined up on one of the beaches. Aiden waves for me to follow him and descends to the beach below. My bare feet hit the warm sand softly. It's been a while since I stood on a beach. I wiggle my toes happily before stepping to the water's edge.

The tide washes over my feet, and to my surprise, the water is warm, like I'd expect it to be somewhere tropical. I catch sight of my reflection in the deep blue water. My eyes are wide and bright, my hair wild and unruly from the flight. I look… different, somehow. I look happy.

"Come now," Aiden calls out from behind me. "Your new home awaits."

Turning, I adjust the bag on my shoulder and eye the dark, dense jungle. I find myself wishing, not for the first time, that I'd remembered to put on shoes. But when we step inside the tangled foliage, the jungle floor is soft. Layers and layers of fallen leaves coat the ground, giving off a wet, earthy smell. The web of trees and plants block out nearly all sunlight. Only a few areas, where the towering trees don't quite touch, let in any light. The rest of the jungle seems plunged into eternal darkness.

Any other time, I'd be terrified. Walking into an unknown jungle with a strange boy doesn't exactly spell out good times in most cases. But oddly, I'm completely calm. Why am I not afraid? Is it because I've spent the past seventeen years reading stories and watching movies about magical places like this? Playing at magic? Imagining what life would be like if places like this truly existed? Places that I could escape to, escape from the sad, pathetic life I've lived until this moment. Is that why I was so quick to believe? So quick to drop everything and come here? I don't know the answer. All I know is that I haven't felt this happy, this at ease, in a very long time.

After what feels like a long walk, the jungle starts to open up in front of us, revealing a large clearing. At first, I think it's empty. But then I look up. High up in the trees, a group of treehouses connected by a network of rope bridges hang suspended. Each treehouse is built around the trunk of its own massive tree. The roofs are made from some of the largest leaves I have ever seen, while the walls are fashioned from random bits of driftwood and fallen branches. Woven palm frond curtains serve as the doors.

But one treehouse stands apart from all the others. It is at least twice the size, and clearly more well-built. The walls are made of some sort of very dark wood. It reminds me of the pirate ship we flew by not long ago. Tightly thatched mats of palm fronds serve as the roof, and the large entrance is draped with a soft green cloth. It is the only treehouse with windows, each of which have small candles burning on the sills. As soon as I see it, I know it belongs to Aiden.

Everything in the clearing is quiet, which strikes me as odd. I expected chaos from the descriptions of the lost boys I've read. But then, Aiden whistles one short, sharp note. Out of each of the treehouses, small figures begin to appear. Dirty little faces peer around curtains and tree trunks. Some look scared, some curious, while others scowl. A small ball of light shoots out of one of the windows in the biggest treehouse.

Tatiana, in her tiny fairy form, zooms over to Aiden, circling his head like a bug around a light. She stops in front of my face long enough to stick her tongue out at me before perching on Aiden's shoulder.

"Don't mind her." He winks at me. "Fairies are so small that they can only have one emotion at a time. Right now, she's quite angry with you."

My cheeks flame. "Why is she angry with me?" I ask hesitantly.

"Because you wouldn't come with her the night she visited. She feels that you wasted her time." He shrugs.

I look at the tiny fairy dangling her feet over the edge of his shoulder, looking at her nails as if she's just had them manicured. "Tatiana, I'm very sorry that I wasted your time. I was hesitant to believe. You understand, right?" I say, stretching up so that I can look into her tiny face.

She sticks her tongue out once more, reaches out one tiny hand, and pulls hard on a thick strand of my hair. "Ouch," I mumble, rubbing my scalp. The little fairy smiles, blows me a kiss, and zooms off into the jungle, leaving a trail of golden light behind her.

Aiden is trying to hold back a laugh, but I'm not entirely

entertained. Maybe fairies *aren't* the sweet little creatures they are made out to be in stories.

"Come, darling," Aiden ushers me into the center of the clearing. "Come and meet the Lost Children."

The Lost Children? I thought they were called the Lost Boys? But as I look around the circle of little faces, I see that there aren't just boys here, but girls as well. Some of the children are small enough to be just toddlers, while others are close to their teenage years. All are barefoot, wearing homemade clothes like Aiden and Tatiana. "Hello," I say softly, giving them a little wave.

The children don't say anything back, just stare at me with wide eyes.

"Children," Aiden's voice booms around the clearing. "This is Elena. She is to be Queen of Neverland!"

A moment of utter silence falls over the clearing after Aiden stops speaking. I look around at the children looking back at me, unsure of what to say or do. Then, a loud cheer erupts from their mouths, making me jump. Beside me, Aiden laughs and takes my hand in his. The children jump up and down, clap their hands, and call my name. I feel a smile spread across my face and tip my head back, laughing at the canopy of green above.

After a minute, Aiden's voice fills the clearing once again. "Alright, alright, quiet down. Elena is tired from her travels and must rest. Off to bed with you lot!"

The children obey immediately. Every single one of them scampers off, climbing up rope ladders and disappearing into treehouses. When Aiden and I are alone in the clearing, he scoops me into his arms and flies me up to his home. In midair, I realize that my whole body is shaking. Not from cold, but from fear.

I'm now alone in Neverland, with no connections to my own world or anyone I have ever known. I'm alone with this strange, beautiful boy who wants me to become his queen. I don't know if I'm ready for something like that. I barely had my life together in the real world. How am I supposed to rule over a magical world and take care of all those children?

I can feel the warmth radiating from Aiden's body as we float up, drawing nearer to the wooden platform around the giant treehouse. The odd, sweet-spicy scent of Aiden's skin fills my nose, intoxicating me as much as his bright eyes.

"No need to be frightened, Elena. I will not harm you," Aiden says.

I can feel his deep voice vibrating in his bare chest. In a few moments, he sets me down gently. The wooden walkway is rough under my bare feet. He holds the green curtain open for me, and I slide past him into the great treehouse, fully aware of how close our bodies are pressed together when I do. Inside, it's warm, almost stuffy. Half-burned candles in each window provide a soft glow to the circular room. I look around, taking in every detail.

The wooden floors are almost completely covered with thick furs. Aiden used large chunks of driftwood to carve a table and two large armchairs. Both chairs are draped with more furs. In the center of the room, the trunk of the giant tree protrudes from the floor and goes out through the ceiling.

But what draws my attention more than anything else is the décor in the treehouse. Small trinkets litter every available surface in the room. Trinkets from *my* world. On the table is a pair of heavy-looking silver candlesticks and a miniature grandfather clock. Small silver jewelry boxes, gold coins, antique compacts, and a set of jeweled hair combs litter the fur-covered floor.

"Where did you get all of these?" I breathe, fingering the jeweled combs.

"Oh, these little things?" Aiden smiles. "Just bits and bobbles I've picked up on my trips to your world."

He says it so flippantly that I can't help but laugh, even though it's clear that he stole them all.

"One man's treasure is another man's trinket," I muse quietly, opening the lid on one of the larger jewelry boxes. A tiny ballerina springs up, spinning to the tinkling music that drifts from the box.

"Please." Aiden gestures to one of the large, fur-covered chairs. "You must be tired. Sit. Rest."

I sink gratefully into the chair. My bare feet ache just a little from the long walk through the jungle, but my body is heavy with exhaustion. Across the room, Aiden pours a cup of steaming liquid from an old painted teapot and brings it to me. "Coffee?" I ask hopefully.

He wrinkles his nose. "Coffee? No. Never cared for the stuff. It's tea."

He may not like coffee, but I have never been a tea person. I inhale the steam rising from the cup. It smells distinctly floral.

"What kind of tea?" I ask, not bothering to try to hide my distaste. He smiles and brushes a strand of hair from my face.

"Tiger Lily tea," he answers.

"I thought Tiger Lily was a person," I say, looking down into the cup to hide the blush burning in my cheeks.

Aiden laughs out loud. "As I said before, darling, you can't believe everything in your stories," he says. "Tiger Lily is a flower, native to Neverland. The tea is made from the flowers; it serves as a wonderful sleep aid," he finishes.

I nod, a bit embarrassed, and take a tiny sip from the cup. Despite its floral smell and my general dislike of tea, it's actually not too bad.

Before I know it, the cup is empty, and my eyes are sliding shut. I try hard to keep them open, but they drop closed anyway. The familiar smell of vanilla and lavender-scented laundry soap fills my nose. I force my eyes open to find Aiden covering me with the blanket from my bag, the one I brought from home. As my eyes drift shut one last time, I hear Aiden's voice.

"Sleep now. For tomorrow, you become Queen."

The pirate stands at the wheel of his ship, thoroughly bored. He wishes that something exciting would happen. Maybe when the boy returns, he will sail to the island and pick a fight. It has been ages since he has been in a proper swordfight, and the darkness is growing restless. Absentmindedly, he steers the ship with one hand, the other hanging uselessly at his side.

A girlish laugh floats on the air to his ears. The pirate's head snaps up, and he sees him, flying right beside his ship. There is a girl with him. A girl with beautiful auburn hair. She waves to the crew as she sails by, giggling, lighter than air. The captain pulls out his telescope to get a better look. When she comes around, flying closer to his position at the wheel, he sees that she is stunningly beautiful. She smiles and waves at him before flying away with the boy.

The pirate's temper flares. How dare Aiden bring such a beautiful girl here, flaunting her about for him to see. He tucks the telescope back into his coat and walks to stand before his crew.

"Well, men," he shouts. "Aiden is back! Who is up for an adventure?" The crew cheers, and the captain turns back to the wheel. A sinister grin spreads across his face as he sets a course for the island.

The boy watches the girl as she sleeps, a smile stretched across his beautiful face. She's the prettiest girl he has seen in a very long time. Much prettier than the last. Maybe even prettier than her. The boy shakes his head. He cannot waste time dreaming of the past. Not when he has Elena in front of him.

There is something different about this one, the boy thinks. Somewhere, deep inside her, a fire burns. A fire that she doesn't even know she has yet. Idly, he twirls the jeweled dagger in his hand while he contemplates what to show her first when she wakes. Maybe the waterfall, or the mermaids…

The boy reaches out to push a strand of hair from her face, and her eyes flutter open for just a moment before closing again. The girl whispers something in her sleep, but he can't make it out. The corners of his mouth tug down. Maybe he can wait a while longer, get to know her… but no. It's past time. The boy will do what must be done. Tomorrow.

SEVEN

When I wake, I recall the most amazing dream. I dreamt that I met a fairy and a beautiful boy, that I flew across worlds to Neverland. But then I realize that it wasn't a dream. I'm *in* Neverland, in Aiden's treehouse. My heart hammers at the realization. I really left London. I ran away with a strange boy in a crown. All of a sudden the circular room is too warm, suffocating almost. I sit up, throw the blanket off my legs and shimmy out of my cardigan. Pushing myself out of the chair, I stretch my stiff limbs. The room is empty, Aiden nowhere in sight.

I move slowly around the room, wondering where he is, looking at all the objects he stole from my world. They all look old, probably from other time periods. As if my thoughts conjured him up, Aiden steps into the room from outside.

"Ah, you're awake. Sleep well?" he asks, stepping toward me. His startling green eyes lock onto me, and suddenly I can't move or speak. He stops mere inches from me, so close that I can smell his strange scent and feel the warmth rippling off him.

"H-how long was I asleep?" I stutter, unable to tear my eyes away from his.

He smiles, his eyes crinkling at the edges. "Most of the day. Don't fret though, you have forever to explore Neverland."

I feel myself nodding, but can't say anything else. All I can do is look deep into his bright, unnerving eyes.

Finally, mercifully, he breaks his hold over me by turning away and setting something on the table. The smell of bacon hits my nose and my stomach responds with a hungry snarl.

"Is that for me?" I ask hopefully. Aiden chuckles softly,

"Of course, it is. Eat, please."

I don't need any more prompting. Rushing over to the table, I sink back into the large chair and dig in. In addition to the bacon, there's eggs and a small chunk of bread and cheese. I stuff the cheese into the slightly stale bread and tear into it. The bacon is crispy and hot enough to burn my tongue, but I don't care. I finish the plate in record time.

Aiden, who stood silently watching as I ate, offers me his hand. "Ready to explore your new home, darling?"

Nodding, I take his hand and let him lead me outside. I'm eager to see the rest of the magical land that I've been brought to. Outside, the clearing is no longer empty or quiet.

The children I met last night are everywhere: running through the clearing, playing games, shouting and laughing. Some of the older kids are tending to a flock of chickens; some are cooking over the fires that light the clearing that seems to be plunged into permanent darkness. Laughter and voices echo off the trees. Small balls of light—fairies—dart back and forth across the clearing, playing with the children. There are more children than I thought in Neverland, probably close to a hundred total.

"Where did they all come from?" I ask Aiden.

He scoops me into his arms and floats to the ground below. "The children? From your world, of course. Some I found in orphanages, some abandoned on the streets, some from cruel homes. They had no one. So, I brought them here," he replies. "See how happy they are now?"

They do look happy. Sure, they might be a little dirty, but they're fed, they have a home of sorts, and they have each other. I smile up at Aiden. "I think it's wonderful that you care for them." His eyes sparkle when I say it. "And where did you come from?" I ask. "Were you born in my world, or have you always lived in Neverland?"

The sparkle in his eyes dulls at my question, his mouth goes tight at the corners. The crown on his head catches my attention. The stones set in it seem to pulse.

"Sorry, I didn't mean to pry," I mumble, looking at my feet and wringing my hands. Aiden says nothing, just looks out over the clearing full of rescued children.

"Are all of those little lights fairies?" I ask now, eager to break the awkward silence.

Aiden's face relaxes. "Of course. The children love them, and the fairies, mischievous little things, enjoy playing with the children."

"Are there a lot of fairies in Neverland?" I ask. I picture Tatiana sticking her tongue out at me and hope that not all fairies are so moody.

Aiden nods. "Thousands. Would you like to see where they live?"

I feel my eyes go wide and my mouth stretch into a smile. Aiden smiles back, his eyes glittering like strange colored jewels in the low light.

"I thought you might." He winks.

He offers his hand to me, and I take it without hesitation, thrilled by the chance to see *thousands* of fairies. I feel like a kid on Christmas Eve. The anticipation of what's to come makes my heart flutter. I feel my feet leave the ground and look down. The clearing and everything in it are fading away, growing smaller as Aiden takes me higher. We go up through the thick canopy of trees. I'm surprised that the sky is dark when we emerge from the jungle.

A huge full moon hangs low in the sky, its reflection rippling across the black ocean. In the distance, a tiny light flickers on the water. Probably the pirate ship I flew over when I arrived—the Jolly Roger. All around us, stars glitter like diamonds woven into deep blue fabric. Aiden tugs lightly on my hand, so I follow him as he leads me over the dark jungle, toward something I didn't notice on the flight in. A massive tree, so tall that it towers over its surroundings. The tree itself looks like it's glowing. As we get closer, I see why. Little balls of light, fairies, flit around the tree, through its leaves and branches, illuminating the whole thing.

"What is this place?" I ask Aiden, my voice thick with awe.

He smiles over his shoulder. "The Fairy Tree. Home to all of Neverland's fairies."

As we approach the great tree, the fairies drift toward us, surrounding us, until we're cocooned in little glowing orbs. It's like floating through the stars, only not as hot.

Aiden lands gracefully on a branch as big around as a normal tree trunk and pulls me close to him. The heat from his body warms me in the cool night. The fairies drift away, congregating in the air in front of us. They form pairs and begin to circle each other. "What are they doing?" I whisper, unable to look away.

"Dancing," he whispers back. His warm breath on my bare skin sends a wave of goosebumps down my cold arms. "It's called the Waltz of the Fairies."

I squint, trying to focus on the pair of fairies closest to us.

He's right; they are dancing. Inside the golden glow of their light, the fairies twirl gracefully around each other, hand in hand. Their translucent wings glitter gold as they beat lightly, keeping themselves aloft. It's the most beautiful thing I've ever seen.

Aiden slides his hand into mine. Reluctantly, I look away from the dance, and am immediately entranced by him again. He looks like an angel in the soft golden glow surrounding the tree—an angel with neon green eyes.

"May I have this dance?" He bows deeply and kisses my hand.

"Yes," I breathe.

He takes a step backward off the branch, hovering in the air in front of me. Gently, he pulls me to him. I creep forward hesitantly, forcing myself not to look down, to keep looking at Aiden, at the fairies dancing around us. One more step, and my feet leave the rough bark of the branch. Now I too am hanging, suspended in the air, floating amongst the thousands of fairies.

We drift farther from the tree, closer to the pairs of fairies, until once more, we are surrounded by them. He lets go of one of my hands, spinning me out away from his body and pulling me back in, close to his chest, closer to him than I've ever been. We spin and twirl, dip and rise, dancing to a music that it seems only I can't hear. The dance ends much too soon. The fairies bow to their partners, and Aiden bows to me. Then they drift away, back to the tree, but Aiden doesn't take me back. Instead, he takes me higher in the air.

"That was amazing," I gush as we rise. "Thank you, Aiden."

"Anything for my queen." He smiles.

"I know I haven't seen much of Neverland yet, but I think the Fairy Tree is my favorite place," I say.

I realize that I haven't once thought of home since I've been here. Maybe this was where I was meant to end up. I can easily just stay here forever, never growing old. No one would miss me. But the faces of Cash and Uncle Henry pop into my mind again. Have they noticed that I'm missing yet? Or will they not even realize it until I don't show up for classes after Christmas?

I shake my head. I have enough things to think about before I make the final decision to stay or go home. For starters, I think Aiden still considers himself a child, but he's not a child. And neither am I. And I still find it strange that someone who thinks they are a child wants a queen. Something about it seems odd, wrong, suspicious. I'm not sure what Aiden's plans for me are, but I need to find out before I agree to stay for good.

"You can visit the Fairy Tree anytime you wish, should you choose to stay," Aiden says, as if he can read my mind.

Maybe he can. I have no idea. I know nothing about him.

"Would you like to see my favorite place?" he asks.

I nod, hoping that maybe I can get some of the information I need to make a decision. Aiden lets go of my hand and flies away very quickly. I realize that this is the first time we haven't been touching since we left the treehouse. Without the warmth of his body, mine is cold, and I find myself wishing that I hadn't removed my cardigan.

"Come on, darling!" he calls from above me. I will myself forward. Without his hand in mine, I become painfully aware that I could drop out of the sky at any time, plummeting to the ground like a stone. But I don't. I float like a helium balloon up into the sky, and follow Aiden to the heart of the island.

After a few minutes, he veers left, then shoots down into the jungle. In a large clearing, not unlike the one the treehouses are in, a large, sparkling lake appears. Mist rises from the surface of the water like smoke from a fire. At the far end, a tall, rocky mountain casts its long reflection on the surface of the water. A waterfall tumbles down over the mountain into the lake. The clearing is loud; the sound of the rushing water echoes off the trees. I slow down, thinking Aiden will do the same, but he doesn't. He keeps flying, full speed, straight toward the waterfall.

My heartrate picks up; my palms grow sweaty. Surely, he's going to stop or veer off to one side. Any second now. But it never happens. He just keeps flying. "Aiden!" I call out, panic rising in my chest. He glances over his shoulder, and I swear I see him smirk, but it does nothing to slow my hammering heart. "Aiden!" I'm screaming his name now. Any second, he's going to slam headfirst into the mountain. A peal of laughter echoes off the trees right before he rockets *through* the waterfall, disappearing from sight.

I let out a breath I didn't realize I was holding. Slowly, I fly forward again, toward the spot where he went through the falls. But instead of going through, I drift to the side of the roaring water, slipping behind the falls. The spray of water dampens my back and chills me to the bone. My teeth start chattering loudly. Behind the falls, a good-sized cave waits, a soft glow coming from inside. I land softly on the rocky floor and step inside.

Aiden is tending to a small fire, tossing sticks on every few seconds. His strange crown is still atop his head, not even crooked. The warmth emanating from the small blaze draws me to it like a moth to a flame. I stick my hands out, warming them and drying my damp clothes. Aiden looks at me across the flames, which cast dark shadows under his eyes. "There you are," he says with a sly smile. "Scare you a bit, did I?"

"That wasn't funny," I huff, inching a little closer to the fire, eager for the warmth. Aiden steps around the flames, and I realize that even though he went through the waterfall, he's still dry. *Magic; it must be.* He comes closer until he can run his warm hands up and down my cold arms.

"Don't be cross. It was only a bit of fun," he pouts. I can see the mischievous twinkle in his eye even in the dimly lit cave. "Nice, isn't it?" he asks, looking around.

"I've never really been a cave kind of girl," I say, trying my hardest to stay mad at him. But his face falls, and I can't keep up the ruse. "But it is surprisingly cozy," I add. He smiles in a way that tells me he knows exactly the effect he has on me.

Wrapping his arms around me, he pulls me in close. "You can be happy here, Elena. You can be happy with me," he murmurs into my ear.

A shiver slides down my spine, and suddenly I can't remember why I had any doubts at all. I lay my head on his bare chest, letting it warm my cheek. "I think you might be right," I whisper.

He pulls away, but keeps a firm grip on my hands. "You will stay, then? You will be my queen?" he asks, his neon eyes bright even in the darkness.

I hesitate, trying to remember why I thought I should go back to my own world. "Aiden…" I begin. But he doesn't let me answer. He dips his head, fitting his lips against mine.

The moment our lips touch, the whole world melts away. His strange, intoxicating, spicy-sweet scent fills my nose. All of the bad memories in my life, all the pain, my world and his. It all fades away until there is nothing left but us—our bodies pressed together, lips moving, his hands in my hair, mine on his chest.

When he breaks the kiss, only one sentence comes to mind.

"Yes," I gasp, struggling to catch my breath. "I'll stay with you."

His face lights up like a string of Christmas lights. He picks me up and spins me around and around until I'm dizzy and giggling. But my happiness is short-lived. About thirty seconds after our lips part, all hell breaks loose.

<hr>

The pirate captain stands under the shade of a tall tree, watching the spot where the beautiful girl disappeared behind the waterfall. When she screamed the boy's name, it felt like a blade running him straight through. To hear his name come out of her pretty mouth was like torture. A boy like him does not deserve a girl like her.

The pirate turns away, cursing the darkness inside that weaves such thoughts through his mind. The girl will be away from Aiden soon enough. He sets off through the jungle to where one of his crew waits. When the pirate sees his captain approaching, he comes to attention. The captain nods, giving the pirate the signal. The pirate nods in return and takes off at a run to pass it along.

The captain resumes his place under the tree at the edge of the lake, watching, waiting. A few minutes later, the boom of the canon fills the air. The captain smiles. It has begun, he thinks to himself. Seconds later, the boy bursts through the waterfall and flies away.

EIGHT

An ear-splitting *BOOM* echoes through the jungle, making us both jump and release each other as if we had been burned. "What the hell was that?" I shout, my ears ringing. A look of pure rage has twisted Aiden's beautiful face.

"I believe we are under attack," he hisses through clenched teeth. "Stay here!" he commands, then disappears though the waterfall.

"Wait!" I shriek. But there's no answer. Aiden is gone, and I'm alone in the cave.

I try to fly after him, but no matter how much I will it, my feet stay planted to the rocky cave floor. I'm trapped here. Another explosion shakes the ground, making dust fall from the roof of the cave. A million questions roll through my head. Why did Aiden leave me here? Who is attacking? *Why* are they attacking? But there's nobody to answer them.

Another explosion, closer this time. Small rocks break loose from the mountain, tumbling into the water in a chorus of splashes. A startlingly awful realization dawns on me. This cave could collapse, trapping or even killing me.

Another explosion, then another, and another. They're happening faster now, closer together and closer to the cave, as if whoever is behind it has set off a chain reaction. But then everything goes quiet. I breathe a sigh of relief. I can't hear anything—the jungle is completely silent, or maybe the explosions just deafened me. My body is starting to relax, the tension leaving my shoulders slowly, knowing that Aiden will be back to retrieve me soon. But out of nowhere, the biggest and loudest explosion yet hits the top of the waterfall, right above me.

Rocks and boulders the size of small cars crash down at the same time my fight or flight instinct kicks in. Before I can think about what I'm doing, I'm running the few steps to the mouth of the cave, diving through the waterfall, into the freezing lake. When I surface, rocks are still falling, raining down all around me. I kick my legs furiously, trying to get away to avoid being crushed.

But I'm not fast enough. A chunk of rock falls on me, hitting the back of my skull with a loud crunch. My vision goes black. Somehow, I know that I'm losing consciousness. My head slips beneath the water. I open my mouth to call for Aiden, to call for help, but all that comes out is bubbles.

And then there's nothing but darkness.

* * *

The boy bursts through the waterfall, the bubble of magic he cast around himself protecting him from the cold water. That damned pi-

rate bastard, the boy thinks, his teeth bared like a feral animal. He had known that the pirate would come for Elena, but he thought he had more time. The boy sails over the trees, heading for the pirate ship at anchor in the cove. The cannons along one side of the ship are firing on the island in rapid succession, as quickly as they can. The boy roars with anger as he descends upon the ship crawling with filthy pirates. Above, the sky turns a deep grey, the wind picks up, and lightning strikes the surface of the roiling sea.

Aiden smiles a sinister, deadly smile. The captain should have known better than to attack his island. He knows the gifts the boy possesses—how he can bend Neverland to his will. It was a foolish mistake on his part.

Aiden lands on the deck, his jeweled dagger already in his hand. Grabbing hold of the nearest pirate, the boy plunges his blade into the pirate's heart, dropping him to the deck with a thud. He cuts his way through the chaos until he finds the massive man he knows is the captain's right-hand man.

The captain waits until the boy has passed before he ventures from his hiding place under the ancient tree. He smiles. Everything is going according to plan. The captain makes his way around the lake, toward the cave he knows lies behind the waterfall. The cannon fire is getting closer. He knows he must get the girl out before the cave collapses. Another hit, then another, and then nothing. The captain pauses, wondering what is happening on his ship, why the cannons have stopped. The boy must have gotten there more quickly than he anticipated.

The captain quickens his pace, stepping over slippery, moss-covered rocks. Suddenly, the cannon fire begins again. One of the heavy cannons balls rips through the jungle, embedding itself in the side of the mountain right above the concealed cave. The waterfall sputters as the mountain splinters, and rocks and boulders rain down into the lake below.

"No!" the captain roars as the cave crumbles, falling into itself, crushing everything in its path, including the girl. He slams his fist into the nearest tree. The knuckles split open, and blood trickles down his hand.

But then, in the middle of the lake, the girl's auburn head breaks the surface. She's alive, the captain thinks. But a chunk of rock the size of a small melon falls, hitting the girl on the back of the head. She goes under and doesn't resurface. He curses, stripping off his heavy coat and boots. The sky above has turned black; thunder rumbles through the clouds. The captain curses the boy as he dives into the water.

⚬⚬⚬

Why does death hurt so much? I think, just before my eyes open. But when they do, I realize that I'm not dead. I'm still alive, staring up at a black sky full of roiling clouds. I try to move, but my limbs feel like they're made of lead. My throat and eyes are on fire. My skin feels tight and dry. I try to speak, to call out for help, but my voice is gone, replaced by a raspy moan.

I hear something nearby. A voice, deep and rough as sandpaper, but with the same lilting accent as Aiden. Aiden; it must be him. I try to call his name, my throat burning with the effort, but can only moan. The voice is coming closer. A face appears over mine, blocking out the stormy sky above. It's a beautiful face, even more beautiful than Aiden's, and I find myself looking up into the most stunning blue eyes. Eyes so blue, I could drown in their depths.

"There, there lass. Don't try to speak," the face says. The rough, sandpapery voice I heard belongs to the beautiful face I see now.

Large, strong hands lift me to a sitting position. One hand leaves my back and reappears in front of my face, holding a dented metal cup. The hand brings the cup to my lips, tipping some water into my mouth. I drink greedily, my parched throat soaking up the delicious moisture. I drain the first cup, then another.

The fire in my throat dies, allowing me to croak out one question. "Where am I?"

The beautiful face with the rough voice replies, "Welcome to the *Jolly Roger*."

I can feel myself slipping back into unconsciousness. *If I die now,* I think, *at least I got to see this face.*

The boy flies as quickly as he can, back to where he left Elena. He must get back to her before the pirate steals her away. Not again, he thinks, the wind stinging his eyes as he races to the lake. When he arrives, the cave is gone, collapsed into itself. Elena is nowhere to be found.

The boy's eyes flash, and lightning strikes the top of the mountain, sending a fresh shower of rocks into the lake. The pirate would pay dearly for this.

The pirate looks down at the girl lying unconscious on the deck of his ship. Her beautiful auburn hair is still damp, splayed around her head, which is leaking blood from the blow of the rock. What little clothes she is wearing are soaked though and clinging to her body. He averts his eyes, looking instead at her pale face, her full lips, tinged blue from cold. She is beautiful. The captain knows that he must keep her away from the boy.

His hand reaches out to touch the smooth skin of her cheek, but he snatches it back before his fingers brush her face. What effect will this girl have on him? On his life? How long will he have to keep her on his ship before he can kill the boy? Will he be able to keep the darkness at bay long enough to make her trust him?

So many questions roll through the captain's head, but he does not focus long on any of them. His focus remains on the girl. On her pale face, her small frame. She needs him; she needs to be protected.

"Miles!" the captain bellows over the howling wind. The massive pirate appears at his side in seconds. "Take the wheel, Mr. Miles. Get us far from this cursed island as quickly as possible."

The pirate nods once before turning away and barking orders at the rest of the crew. The captain scoops the girl up, her limp body too light in his arms as he carries her to his quarters.

Sometime later, I wake with no idea where I am or what time it is. All I know is that I hurt everywhere. My head is pounding, and my whole body aches at the slightest movement. I feel like I've been run over by a semi-truck. I am at least able to push myself up, though my head spins dangerously when I do. A vague memory of a beautiful face lurks just beneath the surface of my muddled mind. That was just a dream though, wasn't it? It couldn't have been real.

I shake my head to clear it, which only causes more throbbing pain. I touch the back of my head, where it's most tender. There's a large lump at the crown of my head, and my fingers come away smeared with half-dried blood. Forcing myself to look around, I realize that I'm on a large four-poster bed in a large, dark room. The silky red sheets match the heavy red curtains that hang over what I assume is a window, though I can't see any light coming from behind the curtains.

The floor and walls are all dark, glossy wood. A sturdy wooden desk and chair sit to one side of the bed, in front of the red curtains. A jumble of papers is strewn across the desk. Old-fashioned oil lamps provide a small amount of dim light.

In front of the bed, a heavy looking wooden door swings open, making me jump. A silhouette large enough to fill the entire doorway appears. I scoot back, pressing as far as I can into the pillows in a feeble attempt to get away.

"Come," a voice booms. But it isn't the voice I heard in my dream. "The captain is waiting."

I flinch away from the loud sound, smacking my head on the wall behind me. I rub the new tender spot on the back of my head, wondering what captain he could possibly be talking about. Then I remember. I'm in Neverland. I was with Aiden. We were attacked. The beautiful face with the rough voice saying, "Welcome to the Jolly Roger..." I'm on the pirate ship I saw when we were flying in. This must be who attacked: the pirates. And that must mean that the captain this man is speaking of... is Captain Hook.

"Come!" the man in the doorway bellows, louder this time. And this time, I listen. I scramble out of the bed, the wood floor smooth under my bare feet. Slowly, I approach the huge man in the doorway. When he sees that I'm finally obeying, he turns and stomps out, leaving me to follow.

He leads me out onto the deck of the ship. A cold wind whips my hair around my face. I rub my bare arms, wishing I'd never taken off the sweater I brought with me to Neverland. The massive pirate turns right, leading me up a short flight of stairs to the upper deck, where the wheel is located.

There, at the wheel, is the man I saw during my brief bout of consciousness after the attack. The one with the rough, dangerous voice and the beautiful face. The big man who led me here bows to the captain and turns to descend the stairs, leaving me alone with the beautiful, terrifying man.

"Good to see you awake, lass," the captain says, his electric blue gaze locking onto me.

His eyes are every bit as bright as Aiden's, and just as captivating. I can't seem to look away.

"What's the matter? Fish got your tongue?" the captain says with a wry smile..

I manage to tear my eyes from his and take the opportunity

to look him over. He's dressed like I expected a pirate captain to dress. On his feet is a pair of shiny black boots. He's wearing a pair of black leather pants that are so tight, it looks like he's wearing leggings, like the ones I have on. A crisp white shirt pokes out from underneath a heavy-looking black coat with large brass buttons all the way up the front. Gaudy silver and jeweled rings decorate every finger of his right hand. His left hand… well, there is no hand. Only a sharp silver hook. Those striking blue eyes are framed by thick black lashes and black eyebrows. The tousled hair on his head and the scruffy facial hair that covers the lower half of his face are both jet black. The contrast between the dark hair and bright eyes makes him utterly stunning to look at.

"You're Captain Hook," I blurt out.

"I suppose you could call me that," he says, one corner of his mouth twitching up as he looks down at the shiny tool replacing his hand. "I see my reputation precedes me."

I look him over once more. "I thought Captain Hook was supposed to be old," I say, regretting the words as soon as they leave my mouth.

His blue eyes narrow. "Who is spreading these filthy lies?" he demands. "The boy? I'll gut the little monster like a fish!"

He says it with so much venom that I take a step back, despite the urge to laugh at what he said. It sounds so cliché— something I'd expect a pirate in a movie to say.

"N-no," I stammer instead. "It's in the story." Suddenly I'm shaking violently—whether from fear or the cold, I don't know. The pirate captain's face softens a bit. I realize now that not only is he not old, but he is actually very young. Probably not much older than I am.

"Forgive me, lass. I did not mean to frighten you. The boy and I do not get on well," he says, looking out at the sea.

I can tell. I don't say it out loud, but I want to. I want to ask the pirate questions, many questions, but the fear spreading quickly through me stops me. Instead, I stand on the deck of the ship, shivering in silence.

After what feels like forever, he turns his bright gaze back to me.

"What is your name, *girl*?" he asks.

I bristle at being called *girl*. Straightening up to my full five-foot-seven-inches, I square my shoulders defiantly. "I am *not* a girl. I am a *woman*," I say loudly and clearly. The beautiful, terrifying pirate looks me up and down, his eyes resting a beat too long on certain areas.

"Look like a girl to me," he drawls, his blue eyes glittering with mischief.

Instinctively, I cross my arms over my chest. But doing so just humors him more. His smile spreads, wide and white, and my cheeks burn in response. I force myself to uncross my arms and straighten again. Anger is bubbling up inside of me now. I can't let him see how weak and helpless I'm feeling. "Why did you kidnap me?" I demand.

The captain throws his head back and laughs long and hard. The anger inside me is beginning to bubble over. I feel like I might explode at any moment, like a volcano spewing lava. My hands are clenched into fists at my sides.

"Kidnap you?" he crows. "You think I kidnapped you? You should be thanking me, girl!"

"Thanking you?" I shout. Oh no, here it comes. The volcano is erupting—I can't hold it in any longer. "You attacked the island! You almost killed me! And now here I am, captive on your ship, and I should be *thanking* you?" I'm breathing hard now, my fists clenching and unclenching, my teeth grinding together. The captain begins pacing around me. I can see just a hint of anger behind his wild smile.

"Aye. I attacked the island," he begins, circling closer to me. "I saw you fly in with *him*. I know what he wants from you. I was trying to save you! And when I found you, you were half drowned, all alone. Where was Aiden then? *I pulled you from the water. I carried you through the jungle. I saved you!*" he roars, coming to stop in front of me, his face just inches from mine.

His confession, and the proximity to him, catch me off guard. He's even more beautiful up close, with his high cheekbones, straight nose, and full lips. Where Aiden is light, the captain is dark, aside from the impossibly bright eyes. The hero and the villain.

As if he can hear my thoughts, the captain says, "Believe it or not, lass, I am not the villain in your story."

"Then who is?" I ask quietly. "What were you trying to save me from?" I can't drag my eyes away from his. I don't feel like I'm in a trance when I look into the pirate's eyes, like with Aiden. The way I feel when I look into the pirate's eyes is different. My mind is clear, for the most part at least. But there's something about this captain, something buried deep inside him, I think, that is drawing me in. He takes a step closer. He smells like the sea. Like salt and wind, mixed with the heady scent of wine and smoke. It's intoxicating. I find myself wondering what it would be like to be wrapped in his arms.

But then the captain responds to my question with an answer so absurd that it shakes me out of my fantasy.

"Aiden is the villain here, love. He is the one you should fear." He reaches out as he says it like he's going to brush my hair back, but he drops his hand instead.

My mouth drops open. "No. Aiden wasn't trying to hurt me. *You* hurt me. I wouldn't have been drowning in a lake if you hadn't attacked."

His eyes darken. "Tell me you have not agreed to what he wants," he says softly. "Tell me you have not fallen for him." His eyes, now a stormy grey, look almost… *sad.*

"Why would I say no? Aiden wants me to be his queen," I say incredulously. The captain reaches out his good hand to take hold of my chin. He lifts it so that I'm looking into those depthless eyes.

"Oh, you poor, stupid girl," he says sadly. "Do you really think that you are the first girl he has brought here under false promises?"

My mind starts to spin. What is he talking about? Aiden has brought other girls to Neverland? Why didn't they stay? No. It's not true. The pirate is lying. He has to be. "Where are they? These other girls?" I ask out loud.

"Gone, lass," he says, eyes boring into mine.

"But why didn't they stay?" I press him further. Why would any girl in her right mind turn down Aiden's offer?

"They're *dead*, love," the captain replies, the sadness in his eyes growing. "The boy killed them. Every single one of them. He was planning to kill you too, but I got to you in time. I saved you," he finishes, his voice barely above a whisper.

The captain looks at the beautiful girl standing in front of him, her hazel eyes wide at what he's just revealed to her. He hadn't wanted to tell her about the boy so soon. He wanted her to get to know him first, to trust him before he shattered her girlish dreams of being a queen. But that was no longer an option. As soon as he saw her straighten up, as soon as she stood up to him, shouted at him, he saw the fire in her. He knew that he could not keep the secret from her. He did not want to.

He looks into those hazel eyes and sees the fear, the confusion, and he can feel his heart breaking for her. Damn that boy! He managed to wrap her around his finger so quickly! But the captain knows that he will not let the boy have her back. He may have been too late to save the others, but this girl, this beautiful, bold girl... he can save her. And he will save her, at any cost.

The boy paces his treehouse, trying to figure out how to get Elena back from the pirate. He could cut his way through the sorry excuse for a crew easily, but how would the girl react to seeing him that way? No, that will not work. He knows that he must be clever, maybe cleverer than he's ever been, to get her back to the island.

He does not doubt that the captain told her all about the other girls as soon as he got the chance. But will Elena believe the pirate? Or has he done enough to keep her under his spell even while she is away? Only one way to find out…

NINE

What the pirate is saying is insane. Aiden wouldn't hurt me—he wouldn't hurt anyone. He took in all those children; he cares for them. He wants me to stay with him forever. "No," I say, voicing my reeling thoughts. "Aiden wouldn't hurt me, or anyone." I'm not sure who I'm trying to convince, though—the captain, or myself. There's something niggling at a corner of my brain, a tiny part that is telling me that he is right, that Aiden is the villain. Could Aiden really have brought other girls here? Promised them that they would be his queen? The sadness in his eyes is almost too much to bear. Surely, he isn't that good of an actor.

The pirate holds up his hand, the one that is just a hook now.

"Aye, love. He would," he says. He spins on the heel of his boot and walks to the ship's railing.

I hesitate before following, but only for a second. Joining him at the railing, I look out across the dark water. The sun is just beginning to rise over the horizon, turning the edges of the sky pink. I turn my head to look at the captain, only to find him staring at me. Curiosity now mingles with the sadness in his eyes.

"How did it happen? Your hand?" I ask. I know that I shouldn't, but I can't help it.

"Do not concern yourself with the details. Just know that the boy is not who you think he is," he replies.

"Are you going to take me back to him?" I ask.

"No," he says, looking away.

"Why not?" I demand. "I want to go back. I don't believe that Aiden would ever try to hurt me. I don't believe anything you say."

"Because you've got a fire in you, love. And I am not quite ready to see it go out," he says, turning his body toward me. He closes the small distance between us and lifts my chin again until I think he's going to kiss me. And oddly, I kind of want him to. I don't know why, but I feel drawn to him. But he doesn't kiss me.

Instead, he grips my chin in his hand, looks deep into my eyes, and says, "Fire like yours is rare. Beautiful. Do not let him snuff it out. Do not let *anyone* snuff it out. Not ever."

I open my mouth to respond, to ask him what he plans to do with me and why he's looking at me the way he is. But I'm interrupted by the massive pirate who brought me up here. He stomps up the stairs, huffing and puffing. "Captain!" he shouts. "He has come for the girl!"

The captain releases my chin and, turning to the giant pirate, begins barking orders. At the other end of the ship, the sound of metal clashing against metal floats eerily across the air.

"Aiden?" I ask, interrupting the captain's orders. I can hear the hope in my voice. I glance at him, afraid for myself, for Aiden, but the hurt on the pirate's beautiful face takes my breath away. Our eyes lock, and for just a moment, I believe everything he said. Then he turns away, facing the men gathering on the deck below.

"Ready yourselves, men! Blood will be spilled tonight!" His voice booms over the wind and the metallic sounds that are getting closer now. His declaration is met by thunderous cheers and the drawing of many blades.

My heart is pounding against my ribs. I don't want to get caught in a battle, but I want to get back to Aiden. I begin looking around for some way to escape. I'm assuming that Aiden is at the other end of the ship, making his way to us. But the ship is huge, and the long stretch between us is filled with pirates who I'm sure wouldn't hesitate to kill me, given the chance.

The captain regards me with bright eyes full of fear mixed with malice. "Get below deck, love," he orders. "I will not let him have you. Not while I am still breathing."

He draws a long, gleaming sword from its sheath on his belt and nods to the massive pirate, who grabs my arm and drags me toward the room where I woke up. The captain charges past us down the stairs, and is lost from sight in the sea of pirates on the lower deck.

I fight the pirate dragging me across the deck, kicking and screaming, but it only slows his progress slightly. Eventually, he gets tired of me fighting and picks me up, slinging me over his shoulder. I look wildly around for Aiden. If I can manage to get free and find him, he can fly us out of here, away from the intriguing captain and his crew of burly pirates. I beat my fists against the massive back of the man holding me. He tightens his grip on my legs, preventing me from kicking. "Let me go!" I scream, my hands tearing at his clothes, trying to scratch his skin.

Then I see him. *Aiden*. At the sound of my screams, his head snaps around, our eyes meeting for a split second before a pirate lunges at him, slicing at him with a long, gleaming sword. Aiden spins away as gracefully as a dancer, cutting the pirate down with a wicked looking dagger. The muscles in his arms and back bunch and stretch, and my heart picks up even more in response. He's breathtakingly beautiful, even in a fight. I was mesmerized from the second I saw him again. When he looks at me again though, his face is twisted with a rage that turns my stomach into a ball of ice.

I gasp. This is not the Aiden that I know. But I realize that I don't know him at all, really. And yet I still want to go to him. *Why?* His bright green eyes are sucking me in, calling to me from across the ship. I make one last attempt at escape. I sink my teeth into the big pirate's back, biting down as hard as I can. He cries out in pain and drops me to the deck. Scrambling to my feet, I start running. Down the rest of the stairs, across the deck, racing toward Aiden.

I dodge around the men that separate Aiden and I, my legs and lungs burning. Aiden turns away from the pirate lying in a bloody puddle on the deck, sees me running toward him, and pushes off, rising into the air. He hovers just above the sea of pirates just out of their reach, holding his hand out to me I'm almost close enough to jump now, to take his hand and let him take me back to the safety of the island.

I push off as hard as I can, my arms outstretched, reaching for Aiden. But hands grab the back of my shirt, pulling me back down. The captain crushes my back against his chest with one arm. I struggle, but his grip is like iron and doesn't ease up, no matter how hard I fight. He presses his hook to my throat. The metal is as cold as ice against my skin. His good hand holds his sword out in front of him.

The pirate captain can almost feel his heart splintering into a thousand tiny pieces when the girl launches herself at the boy. It is a sheer stroke of luck that he is close enough to catch her, to pull her away from the reaching hands of the monster who wants to destroy her. In that moment, the captain knows he will never let that happen.

He presses his hook to her throat, even though he is fully aware that if she struggles, if she escapes his grasp, he will never hurt her. She has not told him her name yet, but it doesn't matter—he will protect her until his last breath. Because the girl with the beautiful auburn hair and hazel eyes makes him feel something he hasn't felt in a very long time. Hope.

Aiden's face twists with rage. "Unhand her, pirate!" he roars. "Or shall I take your other hand?" Mingled with the anger in his eyes is excitement, no fear, unlike what I saw in the captain's eyes before the battle.

He laughs maniacally, his breath hot on my neck, the mix of hot and cold causing goosebumps to erupt on my arms. "I'll not let you hurt her, boy. Not this one. Not again. You can have her only when you can beat me, when you can take her from my dead arms," he growls.

Aiden glances at his dagger, at the pirates circling around him, at the hook threatening to pierce my throat, as if weighing his options. I whimper, fear taking over all of my senses. Aiden's eyes lock onto mine, but they aren't as bright now, like a storm is brewing behind them. The wind begins to howl, swirling around us all, whipping my hair across my face. A bolt of lightning shoots from the sky, illuminating the ship as well as the daylight. The rumble of thunder that follows it shakes the deck beneath my feet.

"You will pay for this, Captain," Aiden hisses through clenched teeth. "The war you have started will be great; much blood will be spilled."

If what Aiden says scares the captain at all, he doesn't show it. His grip on me never loosens, the sword in his hand never wavers.

"That may be," the pirate says. "But the spilled blood will not belong to this girl."

Aiden smiles, a wicked smile full of hate and malice. He raises his eyes to the sky just as another bolt of lightning strikes, closer this time. He looks at me again and says, "Don't worry, darling. I *will* be back for you. Soon." Then he rockets away.

The boy races away from the Jolly Roger, spewing curses and threats on all their lives. If the damn pirate had not gotten in his way, Elena would be here, flying next to him. He saw the longing in her eyes on the deck of the ship, the longing for him. She is still his, which means that the captain has not told her about the others yet, or that he has, and she does not believe him.

Getting her back will be harder than he thought. It is not a job that he can accomplish alone. He will need help, all the help he can get, and time to prepare the fairies and the older children to fight. The boy grins devilishly at the plan forming in his mind. Oh, the cleverness of me…

The captain keeps his hold on me for a few more seconds, then releases me. I drop to the deck, my knees slamming hard into the wood. The adrenaline that was coursing through my veins starts to run out, and now my body is shaking violently with cold and fear.

Next to me, he sinks to his knees, draping a rough blanket

around my shoulders. I cower away, scooting back against one of the ship's masts.

"Don't touch me!" I hiss, pulling my knees to my chest.

The captain stares at me, his icy eyes full of mixed emotions. After a minute, he stands.

"Take her back to my quarters," he orders. "And bring the box."

The last four words grab my attention. Is he going to put me in a box and throw me overboard? No, he said before that he is trying to save me. So what is he talking about? Before I can ask, I'm hauled up and back to the room I woke up in. Inside, I'm shoved down hard onto the bed. I scoot back against the headboard, trying to get as far away from these pirates as I can manage.

The captain enters the room and seats himself behind the big wooden desk. The big man comes next, carrying a large, heavy-looking wooden box. I'm relieved to see that it isn't nearly large enough to fit a body into. The pirate sets it on the desk and leaves, closing the door behind him, leaving me alone with the Captain. My heart rate picks up again. I haven't been alone like this with him, behind closed doors, and it scares me. We stare at each other in silence for a long minute before he breaks it.

"Why did you want to go back to him?" he asks, his rough voice low, dangerous.

"Why do you want to keep me here?" I shoot back. A mixture of amusement and anger flashes across his beautiful face.

"I told you, I am *trying* to save you. But you seem bloody determined to die," he snaps.

I sit straight up, anger simmering just below the surface of my skin. "Aiden wouldn't hurt me!" I shout. "He came for me tonight because you kidnapped me!"

The captain smiles, but it doesn't reach his eyes. "You need proof then, do you?" he asks.

"If you have any," I snap.

He nods once. "Have it your way. Why don't you take a look inside the box?" When I don't move or respond, he urges me on. "Open the box, girl."

I rise slowly from the bed, taking the few steps between it and the desk at a turtle's pace, my eyes never leaving the captain's face. I put my hand on the lid of the box, the wood rough under my palm when I lift it. Inside is a large collection of objects, like the ones decorating Aiden's treehouse. Things from my world.

Scrunchies, ribbons, mood rings, diamond earrings, gold necklaces, compacts, even an old cassette player, are jumbled inside the box.

"What is all this?" I ask, fingering a pink plastic necklace that says 'Best.' Half of a set. The other half would say 'Friends.' I had one just like it when I was little.

"Trinkets from the boy's previous conquests," he says wryly. "I did not get to them in time. That is all that was left of them by the time I got there."

I slam the lid closed, my face burning. "This doesn't prove anything. Aiden's treehouse is full of things from my world. You could easily have stolen these things from him. You are a pirate, after all."

The captain looks like he's considering what I said, then nods. "Aye, fancy things that he steals on his trips abroad. But how do you explain that everything in this box very clearly once belonged to girls like yourself? I saw the way you looked at that necklace, love."

Something inside my brain starts to shift. Could he be telling the truth? Aiden didn't try to deny any of the captain's accusations, even when he said he was protecting me. And he left me here with the pirates.

"Why would Aiden kill all of the other girls? Why would he want to kill me? I agreed to stay with him." But even as I'm saying the words, the pieces are falling into place in my head. What the captain says next just confirms the awful thoughts that are materializing in my head.

"Stupid girl." He shakes his head. "Do you not see? That is how he does it. He courts you, takes you to see the fairies dance, gets you to agree to be his *queen*. Then he takes your life for himself. How else do you think he stays young forever?"

"No…" I whisper. How could I have been so stupid? Apparently, I really need to evaluate my decision-making skills… I left my life, my whole world behind to follow a *murderer to Neverland*. "I never should have left home," I say quietly, more to myself than to the captain.

"That is the first sensible thing you have said since I met you," the captain says, rising and coming around the desk.

I'm speechless, shocked, stunned. Embarrassed at how gullible I've been. How easily Aiden was able to manipulate me. And I fell for it all. Like a fool. I kissed him. I *wanted* him. A wave of nausea washes over me. I grip the edge of the desk, trying to steady myself. The pirate captain steers me around it, letting me sink down into the chair. He crouches in front of me, his hand resting lightly on my knee.

"It's going to be alright, love," he says gently.

It's unsettling how no matter how softly the captain speaks, his deep voice still sounds rough. I force myself to look at him, into those clear, bright eyes. "Take me home. Please," I whisper.

He returns my stare, his eyes filled with pity. "If it were that easy, do you not think that I would have left this hell long ago?"

Tears fill my eyes, blurring his face. He reaches out, his good hand pulling my face toward him until our foreheads are resting against each other. He strokes my hair, comforting me while I sob. After a few minutes, he pulls me off of the chair and into his lap, cradling me against his chest.

"Elena. My name is Elena," I say between sobs. The captain doesn't answer, just holds me tighter.

I don't know how much time passes until I've finally cried myself out, but the pirate never lets me go. My brain and body are overworked and traumatized, so when my eyes begin to close, I give myself over to sleep, eager to escape my situation for at least a little while. And in my dreams, I swear I can smell the sea.

The captain holds the girl, Elena, in his arms as she cries herself to sleep. He knows all too well the feeling of finding out what Aiden is really like. He knows the awful realization of being trapped in this world. Every time Elena sobs, his heart cracks a little more. When she told him her name, such a beautiful name, he thought he might kiss her right then. But he resisted, because she does not want him, she does not feel for him. Why would she? He is just a one-handed pirate with a raging darkness inside of him that he is not strong enough to defeat. But he wants her anyway.

Has he done enough to convince her that the boy who calls himself ruler of Neverland is evil? Has he done enough to keep her from returning to the boy, to keep her here on the ship—with him? Elena's crying stops, and her body goes still as she drifts off to sleep. He wonders if he will be enough. The way he feels around her is something he cannot control, does not want to control. He knew from the moment he saw her flying above his ship that she was special. And as the captain falls asleep, Elena still cradled in his lap, he falls a little deeper for her.

TEN

I wake with the smell of the sea still in my nose. The captain stayed with me all night. He shifted slightly so that he was able to lean back against the desk, but he kept me cradled in his arms. I can hear him snoring softly, his chest rising and falling beneath my cheek. I breathe deep, the smell of salt water and wind surprisingly comforting, and do my best to stay perfectly still—partly because he looks so peaceful and young, not angry and dangerous like when he's awake. And partly because I want to savor this moment, though I'm not sure why.

As much as I hate to admit it, the pirate has gotten under my skin. And while I'm still not sure who is the villain and who is the hero in this story, I feel like I'm getting closer to finding out.

The villain would never have spent the night on the floor holding me, would he? Aiden has left me more than once already. He left me at the waterfall, and again last night. Someone who wanted to spend forever with me by his side wouldn't have left me if he thought I was in danger. *Right?*

The captain stills beneath me. I squeeze my eyes shut, hoping to fool him into thinking I'm still asleep. I don't want him to let me go. I don't want to leave this little bubble of safety that I'm in.

"I know you're awake, love." His rough voice rumbles in his chest.

Lifting my head, I find that I'm looking right into his icy blue eyes. For a second, I forget how to speak. A smile spreads lazily across his beautiful face, and for some odd reason, I want nothing more than to press my lips to his.

He clears his throat, snapping me back to reality. "As much as I'm enjoying this, love, we have things to do. We must be underway," he lilts.

I scramble off of him, then offer him my hand. He looks surprised, but allows me to pull him to his feet.

"Where are we going?" I ask.

"As far away from the boy and his island as we can get," he replies, stripping off his coat and shirt. "He could come back at any time."

I barely hear what he's saying though. I'm too distracted by his bare torso. His skin is smooth and tanned from many hours spent in the sun. His body shows obvious signs of hard work. Defined muscles in his back and arms swell under his golden skin. He turns, catching me staring at his undressed form. My cheeks burn, and I drop my eyes, looking at my feet instead of into his stunning blue eyes. When I peek up at him through my lashes, the sly smile that creeps across his face tells me that he knows *exactly* the effect his half-nakedness is having on me.

After putting on a fresh shirt and coat, the captain comes

to stand in front of me. Using his good hand, he pushes a lank strand of hair behind my ear before pressing his lips to my forehead. I close my eyes, breathing him in, reveling in his touch.

"I'll order a bath drawn for you, and a good meal and some fresh clothes," he says. Then he's gone.

Left alone in the cabin with my thoughts, I pore over all of the information I have about Aiden and the captain so far. As much as I don't want it to be true, I have a sinking feeling that the pirate is right about Aiden. All the signs are there. The flashes of anger I've seen from him, the way he told me he'd been watching me, leaving me when I needed him most, at the waterfall, on the deck of this ship last night. He never denied what the captain accused him of. He only seemed to care that the pirate took me from him. But am I really safe with the captain?

The captain rushes out of his quarters as quickly as his feet will carry him. He needs to get away from her before he gets in too deep. When he caught her watching him dress, he saw the desire in her eyes, the desire for him. He had done his best to make it seem like he was doing it on purpose, but in reality, he had no idea that the sight of him would affect her at all. He could not resist going to her then, touching her. He had gone much too far when he pressed his lips to her forehead though. That was a line that he could not cross with Elena. Not yet, at least.

The darkness inside of him swirls around his heart, surging, looking for a way in. But the girl bathing in his quarters has somehow healed the cracks and chips. With nowhere to go, the darkness sinks down, but not without dragging its claws through his insides. A warning. The captain does not care. Elena is enough to make him want to hold it down.

Less than ten minutes after the captain leaves the room, a large copper tub is brought in and filled with hot water. A plate of food and a stack of clean laundry is brought in as well. My desire to be clean again beats out the hunger gnawing at my stomach. I strip off my dirty clothes and sink gratefully into the tub.

Once I'm clean, I slip on a crisp white shirt from the stack of clothes. It's too big—the sleeves hang well past my hands, so I'm forced to roll them up, but it smells like the sea. It smells like the captain. I use the bath water to wash my own clothes and hang them over the chair behind the desk to dry.

Then, for the first time in what feels like days, I eat. I shovel fruit and bread and cheese and meat into my mouth until I feel like my stomach is going to burst. The captain even sent a jug of wine with the food, which I happily drink.

I've tasted wine before, many times, at parties in my old schools or snuck from someone's parent's liquor cabinet. But this wine is different. It's sour instead of sweet, and strong. After only two glasses, I feel rather tipsy.

I wander around the room, carrying a cup of the sour red wine with me, peeking into drawers, touching the spines of the leather-bound books on the desk and the shelves. Despite all the time I've spent passed out the past few days, unconscious or asleep, I still feel tired. It's like I'm permanently jetlagged in Neverland. I go to refill the cup for the fourth time, but the jug is empty.

After a while, the cabin door opens, startling me. I'm still wearing only the white shirt, as my clothes haven't fully dried yet. I clutch it to my chest and whirl around to see who the intruder is.

The captain is standing in the doorway, his blue eyes wide as they travel down my body, over my bare legs, where the too big shirt clings to my chest. I see his throat bob as he swallows hard. "Feel better?" he asks, his rough voice low and husky.

I nod, painfully aware that my body can easily be seen

through the thin white shirt. The thought of him seeing me, seeing all of me, is terrifying and exciting all at once. I've never let anyone get that far before. That's probably why every guy I've ever dated has chosen someone else eventually. Heat burns in my cheeks. I feel drawn to the captain, like I need to go to him. Hell, I *want* to go to him. And I'm not sure if it's the wine, or just him.

"What are you doing to me?" he asks, so soft it's almost a whisper.

"I was wondering the same thing," I answer, my voice just as low.

And then he's crossing the room, walking fast toward me. I freeze, unsure if it's anger or lust or something else entirely propelling him forward. But then he reaches me, pulls me against him, crushes his lips to mine. He tastes like he smells: salt and wind, wine and, surprisingly, smoke, which is odd because I haven't seen him smoke. I can feel the hard muscles of his chest through his shirt.

The pirate captain kisses me, long and deep, hungrily, urgently. And I let him. The jug of wine I drank has gone to my head—that must be why I let him kiss me. I even kiss him back. As good as it felt to kiss Aiden, kissing the captain is more. So *much* more. Aiden was soft, gentle when he kissed me, like he thought I'd try to stop him. The captain, though… he kisses me with a need, a hunger. With real passion and feeling.

I'm breathless when he breaks away, blue eyes wide with a contradicting look of wanting and bewilderment. I don't want him to stop. I want to get lost in his kiss, to breathe him in forever. And I have a feeling that it's not just because of the wine.

Taking a step back, I reach my shaking hands up and undo the buttons of the oversized white shirt. Then I take his hand, leading him to the large bed. I let the shirt drop to the floor, revealing all of myself to the beautiful, terrifying pirate.

His eyes travel hungrily down my body, but he doesn't

move. The wine has made me bold, brave, so I decide to take matters into my own hands. Slipping his coat from his shoulders, I let it fall to the floor and set to work on the buttons of his shirt. I run my hands over the smooth, muscular planes of his chest, wondering to myself why the universe has been so cruel as to keep this beautiful man hidden away.

"What are you doing to me?" he whispers again, stepping forward and running his good hand up the length of my arm, over my shoulder, to my face, his thumb skimming my lower lip.

I sink down onto the bed, the silky sheets cool and soft under my bare back as I lay down, pulling the captain down with me. And there, on a pirate ship, sailing the oceans of Neverland, we become one.

The captain goes back to his quarters to check on Elena once he has calmed down and gotten his head straight again. But when he opens the door, he finds a half-naked, fully drunk girl poking through his possessions, and all of his calmness is gone in seconds.

His heart hammers in his chest as he takes in her bare legs. The way she looks in his shirt is… more than he can handle. He wishes he had drunk more wine and smoked more of his pipe before coming back here. He says the only thing that comes to his mind: "Feel better?" What a stupid question!

Elena's eyes never leave his face. Not when she nods her response to his ridiculous question, not when he swallows hard, trying not to look at her body, fully visible through the white cloth, not when he risks speaking again.

"What are you doing to me?" he asks her, though he already knows the answer. She is making him feel again. She is making him feel something other than hate and anger. She is making him feel hope and heartache and… love.

"I was wondering the same thing," she says, answering his question.

And then the captain is moving, crossing the room before he can stop himself, going to her, taking her in his arms. He does not think about the consequences his actions might have; he does not think about whether she will stop him or what will happen if he does this.

He does not think about anything but the feel of her skin, the way her body feels pressed against his. He does not hesitate before lifting her chin and crushing his lips to hers. The world around drops away until all that is left is Elena.

The captain pulls away reluctantly. He has no desire to stop, only to keep touching her, kissing her. But he does not want to push himself on her. Elena doesn't speak, just looks at him, the longing clear in her eyes. He wonders if it is obvious in his own. Then, slowly, Elena undoes the buttons of her shirt and shrugs out of it. It falls to the floor, and his mouth goes dry. He does not move when she slips the coat off his shoulders, or when she drops his shirt on the floor next to her own.

"What are you doing to me?" he asks again just before she pulls him down onto the bed, his body on top of hers. But the only response he gets this time is her lips on his.

ELEVEN

The following days on the Jolly Roger pass uneventfully—if one could consider sailing on a pirate ship in Neverland uneventful. Each day, we sail farther away from Aiden and his island, farther out to sea. Will—that's the Captain's real name—never lets his guard down, though. More than once I've caught him watching the sky, searching for Aiden. He knows that eventually, Aiden will come for me. I know it, too. But I also know that Will will protect me.

The morning after I gave myself to him, Will told me that I needed to be prepared and able to defend myself in a fight. We spent that day on the top deck, training with daggers and swords. I'm awful, of course, but Will is confident that I will get better with practice.

The day he taught me about the ship has been my favorite, though. I'm a bit better at that subject. I know port and starboard, all about the sails and rigging. But that's not what made it my favorite day.

Circled in his arms, with his lips caressing the delicate skin of my neck, I sailed the Jolly Roger across the deep blue ocean of Neverland. With the wind whipping my hair and the cool salt spray in my face, it felt a bit like flying. Although his hands on my waist, my hips, his breath warm on my ear as he whispered instructions to me, did nothing for my concentration.

By day, Will is my protector and my teacher. By night, he's my hero, my knight in shining armor, and my love. I learn something new every day, but every night ends the same: tangled in sheets, all bare skin and passion, lips and limbs. I can feel myself falling for him. Falling fast and hard. It scares me, but it excites me too. I don't want to make the same mistake I did with Aiden.

And yet, haven't I already? When I arrived in Neverland, when I was with Aiden, I worried that I was making the wrong choice by staying here, by leaving my world behind. The more time I spend with Will, though, the less I think of the world I left behind. It's barely a memory now. It feels right, being here with him. *He* feels right.

One morning, I wake to an eerie sound drifting in on the breeze through the open window. It's an almost ethereal sounding song—at least, I think it's a song. Rolling over, I see that Will isn't in bed next to me. I sit up, slide off the bed, and pull on the coat he found for me. The sound has gotten louder in the time it takes me to dress. My heart starts to beat faster. Could Aiden finally have come for me? Is this it? No, it can't be. Surely someone would have woken me if that were the case.

I emerge into the dull grey morning light to find all of the pirates, including Will, standing at the railing, looking down at the sea below. I walk quickly across the deck, stopping at Will's side. The eerie singing is louder, so loud that we can hardly hear each other without shouting. Leaning over the side, I see that the water is churning all around the ship. Stretching up on my tiptoes, I lean in close to his ear, so he can hear me better. "What's going on?"

He points to the water. "Mermaids."

"Why are they here? Did Aiden send them?" I ask, staring down into the frothy sea.

Will shakes his head. "I called them." He shrugs. "Aiden has the fairies, so I decided that we needed an ally as well."

A face rises to the surface. At first, I think the mermaid is beautiful. Her long blonde hair and blue eyes are the first thing I notice—until she opens her mouth. Her teeth are like sharp little needles, and there's two rows of them. Her tongue is forked like a snake. On top of the grim look of the mermaid, when she opens her mouth, a shrill, piercing screech fills the air. The mermaid sinks back beneath the surface with a swish of her green, scaled tail. The awful noise disappears with her, morphing back into the eerie song below the surface.

"Are they going to help us?" I ask as a shiny red tail splashes out of the sea a little way from the ship.

"I believe so," he replies, but the wary look on his face makes me think he's not so sure about that.

I touch his arm. "What's wrong?"

He frowns down at me. "Mermaids can be quite vicious when provoked, making them wonderful allies to have during a battle on the sea. But they can be very fickle as well. I only hope that they will answer the next time I call on them."

The mermaids begin to dive deeper, disappearing back into the ocean depths. The song—their way of communicating, according to Will—goes with them. For the rest of the day, an odd silence hangs over the *Jolly Roger*. The air feels charged, like a storm is coming. Will tells me that the crew is not happy about enlisting the mermaids as allies. They feel that they can't be trusted, and that they bring bad luck with them.

To lighten the mood, Will declares that I need to practice with other partners. The crew lines up to have their chance at beating me. Most of them do beat me. I only win a couple fights out of twelve. After the last opponent beats me, I think that we're done, but then Will steps up, his sword drawn.

"One last match, love. What do you say?" he taunts me.

I ready my own sword, but before I can make a move against him, he's there, his blade clashing against mine. My arms shake with the effort it takes to hold him at bay. He breaks the connection, then comes at me again and again until my arms are like limp noodles and I can barely hold the sword up, but I manage to block all of his advances. Will steps back, his sword held behind his back, and bows, congratulating me on a job well done. He kisses my forehead lightly before sending me back to his quarters for my reward, a hot bath.

Muscles I didn't even know I had ache and burn with every step I take on the way to the cabin. Will pushed me harder today than he ever has before. It's like he knows that I'm going to have to test my skills for real, and *soon*. I know, deep down, that I'm nowhere near ready for a real fight. But I have to be. I have to try.

In the cabin, the copper tub is waiting for me, already full of hot water. The sweet smell of lavender rises into the air with the steam. I breathe deep. It smells like home. The world I left behind. My world. The door opens behind me, startling me. Will saunters in, hanging his coat on one of the bed posts.

He raises one eyebrow at me. "May I join you?"

I feel the smile spreading across my face and nod.

After we undress, Will lowers himself into the hot, fragrant water first. I follow, seating myself between his legs, melting into the water, into his chest. He runs his hand absently up and down my arm, causing thousands of tiny goosebumps to erupt on my body. Twisting around slightly, I look deep into his clear blue eyes.

"Aiden is coming, isn't he?" I ask, though I already know the answer, and don't really want to know.

His eyes darken. "Aye, love. I believe he is."

"That's why you want me to know how to fight. You think I'm going to need to," I say, more as a statement than a question.

"Aye," he says again, looking away, out the window at the darkening skies. "There is the chance that I may fall in battle, and you need to know how to defend yourself if that happens."

Despite the heat of the water that surrounds my body, my blood runs cold at the thought of this beautiful man being cut down by anyone, especially Aiden, his equally beautiful opposite.

"We'll win," I say, as firmly as I can. "I won't go back to that island to die for Aiden."

He touches my cheek, takes hold of my chin with his rough, calloused fingers. He looks into my eyes and says, "I will die before I ever let Aiden get his hands on you."

"Don't say that," I whisper, my eyes filling with tears. "I don't know what I'd do if you died."

"If luck is on our side, you won't have to worry about that," he says, still holding my face firmly.

"And if luck *isn't* on our side?" I ask.

"Then you will fight," he whispers against my lips. "You will fight and win and you will go home."

Home… I can briefly recall the rundown old boarding school I moved into in London. The foul smell of the foyer, the rickety stairs, the plain dorm room. I can see my Uncle Henry, the headmaster, and Cash, the boy I met before my trip to Neverland, clearly in my mind. It's sad, that two people I met just a few times and barely know are the only people I picture when I think of my world. Is that place home? I don't think it is. I didn't live there long enough to really make it a home, and nowhere else ever worked out for me either. But here, Neverland, with

Will…

"This is my home now," I tell him. "Neverland, this ship, you…" I trail off, second guessing myself, what I want to say. Will raises his eyebrows, but his mouth turns up at the corners, urging me to go on. I bite my lip, but finish my sentence. "You are my home now, Will." His depthless blue eyes glisten with unshed tears.

"One day, Elena," he begins. "If we make it out of this alive, I—"

But I don't let him finish. I cover his mouth with mine, letting our lips speak silent hopes and dreams against each other.

The boy paces the short length of his treehouse, his brows furrowed. The fairy hovering at eye level shrinks further into the shadows at the edge of the room. "I should not have waited so long," the boy murmurs angrily. "They have gotten too far from the island. Unless I can lure them back somehow… No, that will never work." He has been pacing for hours now, made obvious from the flattened path across the furs. He regrets ever leaving the girl alone in that cave.

The boy stops and lifts his head, his eyes going straight to the fairy. "Fat lot of help you've been," he says.

"What would you have me do?" the fairy asks, cowering away from the strange green gaze. "As you said, they've gotten too far. We cannot possibly all make it there and back again, certainly not if you expect us to fight as well, and with no rest."

The boy considers what the fairy is saying for a few long moments before nodding.

"You may go," he says, turning away with a dismissive wave of his hand. "I will call on you again when I have come up with a plan."

But the fairy is already gone, her light swallowed up by the blackness of the night. The boy begins pacing again, thinking over his options. There must be some way to get her off of that ship. A thought tugs at the corner of his mind. What if…

TWELVE

Late that night, long after Will falls asleep, I'm up, wandering the ship. Sleep never came for me, despite the rigorous training session this afternoon. The faint creaking of the massive pirate ship, the soft snapping of the sails, and the wind whispering across the calm sea are the only sounds tonight. On the main deck, I stand at the left railing. *No, not left, port,* I remind myself, thinking of Will's lessons.

The black night sky glitters with millions of stars. Not for the first time, I find myself wondering if they are the same stars I often gazed up at in my world, or if I am so far away that these are completely different stars. The reflection on the water wavers slightly, despite the relatively calm breeze. I close my eyes, tipping my head back to the sky, breathing in deeply. The familiar smell of salt water and wind fills my nose, calming me.

"Hello, Elena," a voice says from behind me.

I practically jump out of my skin when I hear it. Not because it startles me—well, it *does* startle me—but because I know the voice. The odd, lilting accent, the accent that I've realized is unique to Neverland, the same accent that wraps me in comfort every time Will speaks. But Will's voice is deep, rough. This voice is softer, more melodic. *Aiden.*

Spinning around, I pull the small dagger that Will gave me from its sheath strapped to my thigh. Silently, I thank him for insisting that I keep it on me at all times.

"Well, well, well… Looks like it's a pirate's life for you," Aiden drawls, leaning against the mast.

His arms are crossed over his chest, his legs crossed at the ankles. He looks completely at ease. It makes me furious. Gone is the angelic beauty I saw when I first met him. Now, I can see who he really is. Either that, or he's just dropped the façade now. His ice-green eyes look like they hold many secrets, darker secrets than the ones I know already, and more that I hope I never find out. His smile, once sweet and inviting, now looks malicious, sadistic, evil. I open my mouth to call for help, but Aiden cuts me off.

"Before you scream, why don't you hear what I've got to say?" He smirks, raising one eyebrow in a sort of challenge.

"Why would I listen to a word you say?" I hiss, adjusting my grip on the dagger. My palms are sweaty, and it keeps slipping.

"Because I'm going to tell you a story." Aiden smiles. But his eyes narrow as he says it, making him look even more menacing.

"A story?" I ask. I can hear the doubt and wariness in my voice.

"Yes, darling, a story. One about two brothers who ended up in Neverland, trying to escape being drafted into a great war.

The brothers were happy. They were free in Neverland. For a while," he begins.

My heart starts to gallop inside my chest like a horse on a racetrack. My mouth feels like it's been stuffed with cotton, but I do my best to keep my face passive, unreadable. I won't let him see the way he affects me, though I know, deep down, that I'm not going to like this story.

Aiden looks a little disappointed when I don't say anything, but he continues on with his story.

"One of the brothers fancied the island. The other, the sea." Aiden circles me as he talks. "One brother learned to fly and to do magic. The other brother built a great ship and learned to sail. Then, one day, the magical brother ventured back to the real world, in search of companions to join him on his island, for he had grown lonely without his brother's company. He was kind and thoughtful, so he brought back a crew to help the pirate brother sail his ship across the Never Sea. For himself, he brought a girl. A beautiful English rose, Wendy."

Aiden is circling closer and closer. I turn in a circle with him, careful to never turn my back on him.

"Wendy and the magical brother were deeply in love, meant to be, *soulmates*. But the pirate brother was jealous of them, of their love. He wanted Wendy for himself. So, he took her.

"The pirate stole her away in the dark of night while the island slept. He tried so hard to keep her from the magical brother that he killed her in the process. The magical brother was distraught. He banned the pirate brother from the island and tried to fill the hole left in his heart by bringing children to the island. Lost children who needed caring for. But it was not enough. The magical brother longed for his Wendy, but she was gone forever, thanks to his brother.

"Since then, the brothers have been at war, and every time the magical brother brings a new girl back to the island to try to replace Wendy, the pirate steals her away and murders her. Just like he murdered Wendy," he finishes, stopping so close that I can smell the spicy, sweet scent of him that I can never place.

My heart is hammering against its cage, trying to break free, to get away from Aiden. I already know the answer, but I speak anyway.

"If you're the magical brother, then that means that Will is…" I trail off, unable to bring myself to say the words.

Aiden smiles down at me. An evil, wicked smile that makes me want to scream. Makes me want to rage against him, pound my fists against his chest, his face, drive my dagger into his heart. But I don't do any of those things. I'm frozen in place, not from fear, but from shock.

"Yes Elena, he is the pirate brother. *My* brother, Will."

"No," I whimper, blinking away the tears that are filling my eyes, blurring my vision.

"I can see by your reaction that my dear brother's story was a bit different, wasn't it?" Aiden sneers down at me.

A sob escapes my lips, I can't stop it. I close my eyes, the hot tears spilling down my cheeks. I wipe them away, but when I open my eyes, Aiden is gone. I'm shaking violently, gasping for air. Will told me a bit about his past, not long after our first night together. But he never mentioned that Aiden is his brother. He never mentioned Wendy, or her murder.

How could he not tell me? I've asked him more than once how he ended up in Neverland, why he and Aiden hate each other so viciously that they are willing to kill each other. But his answer is always the same. "The details don't matter," he tells me every time. But he was wrong. So wrong. The details definitely do matter. Especially now.

If Will—no, I can't even call him that anymore. Not if the story is true. Not if he lied to me about everything. Captain, then. If the *captain* is really who Aiden says he is, if he did *murder* Wendy out of jealousy and lust, then… I don't even know what will happen then. My brain simply cannot imagine it.

The boy laughs to himself as he sails through the night air, thinking of how smart and clever he is. His plan worked beautifully. His story about the two brothers was just the thing he needed to create a rift between the girl and his brother. A rift large enough that he is sure he will be able to go back tomorrow night and retrieve the girl. Then he will finally be able to perform the spell, to make her his queen.

He waited far too long in between queens. He can feel his magic weakening each day that passes. He can feel himself… aging. The boy shoves the nasty thoughts from his mind, choosing to focus on the joy he feels when he thinks of the look on the girl's face at the end of his story. The tears she spilled when she realized who the pirate really is. The boy reaches his little house in the trees and sprawls out on top of the furs. Sleep comes easily for the clever boy tonight.

I don't remember walking across the deck, or going down the stairs, but somehow, I make it back to the cabin. Will wakes when the door shuts behind me, blinking sleepily for a few moments. His eyes clear after a minute, but then panic settles over his features. He launches himself out of the bed, crossing the room quickly.

"What's wrong, love? What's happened?" He tries to take me into his arms, to gather me against him, but I shove him away. Now he looks confused, hurt. But I don't care.

"Elena, what is the matter?" he asks again, his voice shaky.

I keep my hands up, to keep him away, and realize that the dagger is still clutched tightly in the right one. When I look into his fathomless ice-blue eyes, eyes that I now see resemble Aiden's so much, the hurt I see in them is almost enough to make me forget what Aiden told me. *Almost.*

"Is it true?" I ask. The tears begin to dry on my cheeks, burned away by the rage simmering inside of me now, looking at Will, thinking of how he lied to me for weeks. "Is Aiden really your brother? Did you *murder* Wendy?"

"Elena, I can explain," he whispers, taking a step toward me.

I raise the dagger, trying to keep my hand from shaking. "It is true!" I hiss, the anger surging in my chest at the confirmation of my worst fear. "You wanted Wendy, but she loved Aiden, so you killed her!" I'm shouting now, the anger and pain building in my chest with each gasping breath that I take.

"Do you truly think so little of me, Elena?" Will asks, his voice quiet, dangerous.

"Tell me it isn't true," I demand. "Tell me you didn't murder Aiden's girlfriend because you were jealous!"

Will throws his arms up. "I did not murder Wendy!" he shouts. "I was trying to save her! During the rescue, she got caught in the crossfire. Aiden shot an arrow right into her heart and blamed me for her death!"

"Why should I believe you? You didn't even tell me that you and Aiden are *brothers*!" I cry. He doesn't respond, just stares at me with those eyes that I love looking into. The thought of it makes me sick now. "Nothing?" I laugh bitterly. "I guess that's what I get for jumping into bed with a pirate."

I turn away, but not before I see his face twist with pain at my venomous words. I have to stop myself from turning back, from going to him and apologizing. Instead, I snatch a pillow off of the bed and slip my feet into the worn pair of boots I got from one of the men. Refusing to say another word, to even glance at him, I stalk out of the room, slamming the door behind me.

No tears fall while I walk up the stairs to the upper deck. None fall when I toss my pillow onto the smooth wood, or while I roll from side to side, trying to get comfortable. But when I finally close my eyes, I can't stop the tears that flow freely no matter how hard I squeeze them shut.

The pirate stands frozen in his quarters, staring at the door that Elena slammed behind her, willing her to come back, to open it and come to him. But the door stays closed, and the darkness that he has pushed so deep inside of him begins to rise up. Damn that Aiden! he thinks. Damn him to the depths of Hell! He should have known that the boy who calls himself the King of Neverland would have made one last attempt to turn Elena against him.

The pirate curses the boy for getting past him, for getting so close to her without him knowing. He should have been there to protect her, but he had let his guard down. And this was the result. Of course, he could have told her his side of the story a hundred times over the past few weeks and avoided all of this completely. But he did not. The pirate wonders if he kept the truth from her because he was trying to protect her, or if he was trying to protect himself.

The darkness surges up his throat, threatening to spill out and unleash the monster he keeps so carefully concealed. He should sail back to that cursed island and gut Aiden like a fish for coming here and filling Elena's head with his twisted stories.

He pushes it down, trying to keep it at bay, to clear his head of such dark thoughts. Elena would not believe him any more if he sliced his brother open from neck to naval. It would likely only fuel her hatred for him.

The pirate stares at the closed door for a minute longer before sighing, walking around the desk, and sinking into the chair. He knows he will not get any sleep tonight, but he will leave Elena alone to cool off. He will stand guard all night while she sleeps, and tomorrow, he will tell her the real story.

I wake to the sound of shouting coming from the lower deck of the Jolly Roger. I can't understand what they're saying due to their thick accents. Rolling over, I grimace at the ache in my lower back from sleeping on the unforgiving deck. When I sit up, my head throbs with an impending migraine. Not for the first time, I wish I had never come to this place. Never met Tatiana the fairy or Aiden or Will.

I should have stayed in that rundown school in my own world, where everyone might be liars and backstabbers and generally awful, but at least they didn't have magic or secret agendas to kill me to stay young. Struggling to my feet, I stretch my arms up over my head and bend at the waist until my fingers brush the deck of the ship. My lower back gives a sharp pang of pain. When I straighten, I glance around for Will, but don't see him on the deck with the rest of the crew, who are hurrying around, performing their daily tasks.

Good. I don't want to see him or talk to him anyway. What I want, what I *need*, to do is figure out how to get the hell out of Neverland and back to my own world. There's a tiny part of my brain that disagrees with me, showing me images of Will's stunning face, of the memories I've made with him on this ship. I shove it down, willing away any good thoughts about this place and the people who inhabit it.

I set off down the stairs, hoping that there is still some food left over from breakfast in the galley. Down a second set of stairs, into the belly of the ship, a left at the crew's quarters—where all of the hammocks and cots are empty now—and into the narrow galley where the cook prepares the meals.

Not one man gives me a second look or even glances my way. They've all grown used to seeing me around, wandering the ship, training with swords and daggers. None of them suspect that Will and I are on the outs. Or if they do, they don't let it show.

There's not much left over from breakfast, just a few pieces of dry toast and an untouched bowl of tropical fruit gathered from the island. *Fine with me,* I think. *Let them all get scurvy.* I will happily eat the fruit they choose to waste. Sliding onto one of the rough wooden benches, I nibble at a piece of the flavorless toast and help myself to the bowl of assorted fruit, most of which I have never seen before. There's bananas, some kind of round, purple, sour-smelling fruit the size of a coconut, and what I thought was a mango, but when I sliced into it, the insides were not yellow, but bright red.

Sure, it's not a lavish breakfast like I've gotten used to eating in Will's quarters, but it's perfectly adequate. As I eat, I mentally list all of the possible escape scenarios I can think up. I could go back to the island, to Aiden, pretending that I'll give in to his sick, twisted desires. But in reality, I'll only be there to find the pixie dust that will allow me to fly, and then I can fly home.

The downfall with this plan is that I'm not sure I can make it back to my world on my own. I had Aiden guiding me when I first came here, but the journey through the stars was... hectic. There's no guarantee that I won't end up somewhere else, *somewhere worse.*

Maybe I can find a fairy, one who will help guide me home. Tatiana isn't an option; she would probably just sell me out to Aiden. But maybe some of the other fairies aren't as close to him—maybe one of them thinks what he plans on doing to me is cruel, wrong. Maybe one of them will help me.

All I would have to do is make it back to the island, go to the fairy tree, and plead my case without being detected by Tatiana or Aiden. It will be difficult, and dangerous probably, but it's definitely an option I will keep at the front of my mind unless something better pops in.

Hauling my tired body off the bench, I head out of the galley and into the small bathing chamber that the crew shares. Its not nearly as nice as the huge copper tub in Will's quarters, but the basin full of lukewarm water and somewhat clean towels will do fine to freshen up a bit. The thumping of heavy footsteps on the deck above echo through the tiny room like thunder. One of those sets of steps could belong to Will.

I could go up and talk to him, try to figure this all out… *No, I think.* I'm better off staying far away from him, from Aiden, from everyone. I wet one corner of the cleanest looking towel and strip off my shirt, wiping the salt and sweat from my skin. Then I bend over the basin, scrubbing my face with the luke-warm water.

I even go so far as to stick my head under the water to rinse my hair. I dry myself off with the rest of the towel and yank my fingers through my tangled hair, since I don't have a comb or brush. Buttoning my shirt back up, I suck in a deep breath before opening the door and strolling up the stairs and onto the deck.

The captain wakes slowly, his arm stretching out across his bed, fingers searching for the warm body that sleeps next to him. But the other side of the bed is unslept in, the silk sheets cold. His eyes fly open to find that Elena never returned to his cabin in the night. The darkness swells inside of him. She chose to sleep somewhere else on the ship, to get away from me, the captain thinks. Hot rage courses through his veins, followed quickly by icy pain. She left me, he says silently.

A weight slams into his chest when he thinks of what she said to him the night before, so heavy that it knocks the air from his lungs. Her beautiful face was so twisted with anger and hurt that he had barely recognized the girl he has grown to love. And he does love her. He loves her with every bone in his body. But he had betrayed her by not telling her about his history with the demon, Aiden. He had hurt her deeply, like all the ones who had come before him.

He should have known that keeping things from her would only ruin everything. Especially after she had told him about the boys she'd loved before, what they all did to her. How they shattered her heart again and again until she had felt she may never be whole again. The captain closes his eyes and covers his face with a muscular arm. He is such a fool. A wicked, bloody fool.

The captain rises from his bed, shivering at the crisp morning breeze filtering in through the open window. He shrugs on a shirt and his coat, steps into his pants and boots, and stands at the basin, splashing the cool water on his face. When he finally has the courage to look at his own reflection in the mirror on the wall, he can only look for a few moments before his mind shouts Coward! again and again until he must look away.

But the captain is not a coward. He is William, captain of the Jolly Roger, King of the Never Sea. He is fierce and strong and cunning. No, he is not a coward. He braces his hands on the table and stares at himself in the mirror, daring his mind to call him a coward one more time. But the voice stays quiet, and he knows what he must do now. Turning away from the mirror, the captain takes a deep breath and stalks to the door, throwing it open and disappearing up the stairs.

<hr>

The boy rolls over on the soft furs, opening his eyes, a smile spreading lazily across his face. He had such wonderful dreams while he slept. Dreams of beautiful girls crying, of shouts and sobs and the ritual that would keep him young for a while longer. Soft green light filters in through the windows, signaling that the day has come. Today he will retrieve the girl; he will finally have his queen.

The boy rises from the floor, stretches his limbs, and heads for the door. There is much to be done before he brings the girl back. But first, he thinks with a grin, breakfast.

Thirteen

I blink a few times after emerging into the bright morning light, my eyes having adjusted to the darkness below deck. The ship is still crawling with pirates hard at work maintaining the course. Some men adjust the billowing and blood red sails, some wash the deck, some scramble into the rigging to check on knots and ropes. I purposely don't look to the upper deck. If Will is out of his quarters, that's where he will be.

Instead, I walk briskly down the length of the ship to the bow, to the spot where the railing on both sides meets in a point. Again, no one looks at me any differently, if they bother to look at me at all. Bracing my forearms on the wooden railing, I close my eyes, breathing in the salt and wind smell that now offers so much comfort and peace to me. I open my eyes and lean as far over as I can, straining to see the haunting face of the exquisitely carved mermaid figurehead that leads the way.

Funny, how whoever carved the mermaid made her beautiful, when in reality, mermaids are dangerous, dark creatures. At least here in Neverland. Who's to say that there isn't a magical land out there where mermaids are sweet and beautiful? If Neverland exists, why can't that world exist too? Maybe I'll go there when I leave this place. Maybe taking my chances with the fairy dust is my best option. Even if I don't end up back in my own world, even if I end up in some other magical land far from here, it has to be better than this. Right?

The captain watches the girl stroll up the stairs from below deck, the bright morning sun turning her auburn hair to red-gold fire. His breath catches in his throat. She is stunning. He knows that he doesn't deserve her forgiveness, her love, her. But he can't stop feeling for her. Not even the darkness surging inside of him can black out the bright light his love for her casts.

Will begins to move from his position at the wheel to go to her, but stops when she walks on without so much as a glance in his direction. It makes his heart ache, the way she is so blatantly ignoring him. But as the thick darkness rises up a bit more in response to the slight, he realizes that he deserves it.

He watches the girl saunter across the deck like she owns it, and a smile tugs at the corners of his mouth. She is so much more than he ever dreamed. When she stops at the bow, he can almost picture her face, her eyes closed, breathing in the smell of the sea. He has seen her do it often enough that he knows the tilt of her head, recognizes it.

Her hair shines bright and fiery, and Will thinks that he may be colorblind to all others. When she leans over the side and her toes come off the deck, he stops breathing. He fights against the urge to sprint the length of the ship, to pull her back, to reprimand her for being careless. She would not want that. No, he corrects himself. She wouldn't want me.

When her feet are planted firmly on the deck, the captain lets out his breath, hoping that she will turn around just so he can see her face. Selfish of him, really. But he doesn't care. And she doesn't turn around. She just keeps staring out across the sea.

My body tenses when I hear the heavy boots on the deck, signaling that Will has finally found me. Part of me hoped it would happen sooner; the other part wished that I would never have to look into those startling blue eyes again. I wait a few seconds before turning to face him, leaning my back against the bow of the ship.

Will looks nervous, and angry, and hurt, but I keep my face blank, a mask of disinterest. His body is rigid, perfectly still. He opens his mouth as if to speak, but closes it, opening it again a second later.

"Do you have something to say to me? Or did you just follow me up here to stare at me?" I ask, my voice as cold as ice. It makes me cringe, to talk to him like that when just last night I was in his arms. But he lied to me. And I've had enough of being lied to.

He opens his mouth again. "Elena, please," he begins.

"I don't want any more excuses or apologies," I cut him off, turning my back on him just so I don't have to see the pain in his eyes caused by my words.

"I did not come here to make excuses, and I am sorry, but that is not what I wanted to say," he says quietly.

I take a deep breath and turn again to look at him, taking in his stunning face, the lean, powerful body I am now so familiar with, those eyes that are so clear and bright, and yet hide so much darkness, so many secrets. "I'm listening."

He nods and moves so that he can lean against the railing next to me. He takes a deep, shaky breath, lifts his eyes to the clear blue sky, and begins talking.

"I should have told you about Aiden. That he was my brother, that I had something to do with the death of Wendy. But Elena, you must believe me. I did not kill Wendy. I knew what Aiden planned to do to her, *why* he really brought her here. He told her he loved her; he tricked her into coming to Neverland. All so he could murder her and use her life to keep himself young for a bit longer.

"I wanted to save her. I did not want my twisted brother to take the life of such a sweet girl. So I stole her away in the night, just as Aiden told you. But his arrow is the one that found its way into her heart, and her death is on his own bloody hands. Ever since then, every time he brings another girl to this cursed place, I try to save her, and every time I fail. Until you."

Will looks up at me with those incredible eyes, now brimming with tears. I have to look away; otherwise, I'll fall back into bed with him without another word. "I know you didn't kill Wendy. I knew that from the start. That wasn't the part of the story I had an issue with," I say quietly, avoiding his gaze.

He stiffens beside me. "I figured as much," he says, his eyes burning holes through my skull.

I wait for him to go on, to tell me why he kept the fact that Aiden is his brother a secret, but all I get is silence. My temper flares. "So that's it., then? That's all you wanted to say to me? Something I already knew. *Wow,* thanks," I say, my voice dripping with sarcasm. Turning, I start to walk away, to get away from him before I say things I don't mean, things that will hurt him even more.

"Elena!" Will shouts behind me. "Damnit, Elena, wait!" The sound of his boots on the deck grows closer.

I whirl around, anger taking over, and begin shouting at

him. "I don't want to hear about Wendy, or the other girls, or what happened to them. What I want to know, *no*, what I *need* to know is why you lied to me! Why did you keep secrets from me? I gave you everything! And all I got was lies and secrets! You didn't even tell me that Aiden is your *brother*," I shout.

"Because I do not think of him as my brother, Elena! He is nothing but a shell of the man my brother, Aiden, was!" A single angry tear rolls down his cheek.

I know as soon as I see it who is telling me the truth, and who has deceived me yet again. Without willing myself to go to him, somehow, I'm in Will's arms.

"I'm so sorry, Will. I knew, deep down, I knew he was lying. But I've been hurt so many times, I let the fear cloud my judgement. Please forgive me, Will. I'm so sorry!" I sob, my tears running down his bare chest.

He strokes my hair, whispering reassuring words in my ear. "It's alright, love. It's alright."

He holds me close, lets me weep into his chest, lets me cry myself out. His arms never loosen their hold around me; he never wavers. Will is my rock in the middle of the sea that surrounds us. He has been since I met him. Maybe even before that, since I arrived in Neverland. I've shed all of my tears, and I look up to gaze into his eyes, to tell him something. But I don't get the chance.

The boy is impatient. He does not want to wait until nightfall to retrieve his prize. All morning long, he tries to keep himself occupied, hunting the wild pigs in the jungle, helping the smaller children herd the chickens into their makeshift coops, harvesting vegetables from the gardens. But she is always there, in the back of his mind, beckoning to him from far off in the sea. Elena.

The boy has run out of things to do by late morning. His plans are solid; the fairies are prepared for what he has ordered them to do. All that is left to do now is wait. But the boy is sick of waiting. A shudder ripples through him, stopping him from his pacing. Another effect of the magic that flows through his veins, twined with his blood, fading away. If he does not act soon, he will not be strong enough to do the ritual that will bind him to Elena.

Aiden storms from his treehouse, yelling for someone to get a fairy here now. When the tiny blonde fairy arrives just minutes later, the boy is struggling to leash his temper, the anger and fear almost too much to bear. It takes all of his restraint not to tear her wings off and toss her broken body to the jungle floor.

"Gather your friends," Aiden hisses instead. "We move now."

The captain looks down at the girl, once again safe in his arms. He takes in her lovely face, the hazel eyes gleaming with tears, the fiery hair that whips around her. I will never tire of looking at this beautiful creature, he thinks. When she buries her head into his chest, tears flowing freely, he just wraps his arms tighter around her, shielding her from all the bad in the world.

He had regretted going to her, the feeling growing with each step he took across the deck of his ship. Regretted it more when she all but dismissed his plea of innocence, when she shouted and screamed at him, when she turned away from him again. But when her eyes filled with tears and she ran at him, flung herself into his embrace, he realized that not going to her when he did would have been the biggest mistake of his life.

Elena continues to cry, her sobs muffled by his shirt, and he lets her. Because it is what she needs him to do. She needs him to protect her, to console her, to love her. And he does love her. Despite all of his reservations about falling for her so quickly, despite the fact that he has not felt love since his brother turned himself into a monster many years ago. He loves her.

Elena's tears finally stop, and she pulls away just enough to tilt her head back and look up into his eyes. But she does not get the chance to say whatever it is she is thinking.

Above the Jolly Roger, the boy circles like a bird of prey, his eyes searching the crowded deck for her. The pirate bastard is not at the wheel as he usually is, but he must be on deck somewhere, the girl as well. Surely, they are not off somewhere sulking about the quickly squashed romance between them. The boy smiles at the memory.

His body shudders, his teeth clacking together. The spasms are coming more frequently, growing stronger. He must hurry. But he still has not located the girl, or his brother. He risks flying lower, to better see the full expanse of the great ship. There. Aiden smiles, catching a glimpse of the girl's bright hair.

The boy begins to descend, hoping he can get her off the ship without being detected. But wait, the girl is not standing alone at the bow of the ship anymore. His brother is there now, pleading for forgiveness by the looks of it. From where he hovers overhead, the boy hears the pirate's voice rising, and Elena's rising to match it. Good, he thinks, let them keep at each other's throats. It will make the task of taking her easier if she is still angry at the pirate.

But then, then… the girl launches herself into the arms of the pirate. Into the arms of his brother. The pirate strokes her hair and holds her close to him. Jealousy and rage spike in Aiden's veins at the sight of his bastard brother and his queen locked in such an embrace. His eyes flash, and the skies begin to darken, the storm blowing in on a wind of his own making. Magic crackles through his veins and at his fingertips, dancing like the lightning striking the ocean beyond.

FOURTEEN

A giant ball of fire blasts through the hull of the ship, narrowly missing us before crashing through the opposite side. The force of the double impact tears me from Will's arms, throwing me back into the wooden railing. I hit it hard and fall to the floor. My head is spinning. Something warm is trickling down my face. When I touch it, my fingers come away red.

The air is filled with smoke, and splintered wood is everywhere on the deck, raining down from the sky. Debris is lifted into the air by a wind that wasn't blowing just minutes ago. I can't see Will anywhere. "Will!" I scream. "Where are you?" My lungs and throat burn from the thick black smoke billowing out of the gaping hole in the ship. I can barely see through it.

Small fires have started in different places on the deck, sparked by the initial blast and blowing debris. The wind turns cold and blows harder, bringing with it the screams of the crew, more smoke, and the smell of burning flesh. I gag at the smell, at the sounds coming from all around me, at the pain in my head.

Then I see him. Will. He's lying about a hundred feet away, a long, sharp splinter of wood protruding from his chest. His head hangs limp to one side. He's not moving. I run to him, sure that when I reach him, his heart won't be beating. I dodge one of the smaller fires that has sprung up, finally coming to a halt in front of his limp body.

The first thing I do is check for a pulse. It's there, but weak and irregular. The piece of wood went through his right shoulder. It missed his heart and any other vital organs I can think of. But who knows what kind of internal damage the blast may have caused?

I have to get the wood out. My eyes are watering, stinging from the smoke. My lungs burn like the fire that ripped him from my arms. Forcing myself to focus, I look around, find a partially burned scrap of cloth tangled in a coil of rope, and wrap it around my hands. I pull on the wood as hard as I can. It takes a few minutes, but finally, it comes free, slicing through the dirty rag and cutting into my palms. I fall to the floor, knocked off balance by the force of my pull.

Flipping over onto my knees, I start crawling over to where he's lying. I pat his cheek, trying to wake him. "Will," I shout, hot tears mixing with the blood and soot on my face. "Will, wake up!" Through the gaping hole in the side of the ship, I hear nothing but chaos—screams and splashes and an unsettling ripping sound. Even if I call for help, nobody will hear, nobody will come. I try to shut out the panic and the fear.

"Will!" I yell, pounding on his chest. The panic begins to take over my body, laboring my breathing, making my heart beat too fast. Aiden is out there, somewhere in the chaos. He is going to come for me, and I won't be able to stop him. My dagger, the one Will insisted I always keep on me, is gone, the entire sheath ripped from my thigh in the blast. If Will doesn't wake up, I'll be completely defenseless. I pound on his chest again, tears streaming down my face, dripping onto his skin, my blood and sweat and tears mixing with his. I'm about to give up, to try to find a way to save myself, when he groans softly.

"What the bloody hell happened?" he asks, his eyes fluttering open. He tries to sit up, winces, and lays back down. "That bloody *hurts*," he groans, his hook prodding gently at the torn shoulder.

"Will! I thought I'd lost you!" I cry out, collapsing onto his chest. It makes him wince again.

"Easy," he warns. "I'm a bit worse for wear at the moment."

But when I raise my head and our eyes meet, his face crumples and he pulls me down to him.

"Don't worry, love. I'm a survivor. It'll take a lot more than a glorified splinter to do me in."

"Good to know," a voice smooth as silk says from behind me.

Aiden. The insane amount of adrenaline and fear coursing through my veins is the only thing keeping me focused right now. It will be the only reason I survive, if I do survive. I don't even turn to look at Aiden, to acknowledge his presence. *Can you fight?* I mouth to Will. He shakes his head and takes my hand.

"No. But you can." He gives my hand a little squeeze. "Fight, Elena. Fight hard. Do not let him take you." He brings my hand to his lips and brushes them over my knuckles.

"I will *not* leave you," I say, trying to stop the sobs racking my body.

"But you must. Just know that… that I love you. Now, and always."

A gasping sob escapes from my mouth as I throw myself

down, molding my lips to his for what could very well be the last time. "I love you, too," I whisper against his lips.

A searing pain spreads across my scalp. Aiden is pulling me off of Will, dragging me across the debris-littered deck by my hair.

"How touching!" Aiden sneers. "My dear brother, William, and my queen, Elena."

I try to struggle, to escape Aiden's grip, but the pain in my head is too much. I can feel the hair being ripped from my scalp. "I will *never* be your queen," I hiss through clenched teeth.

"But Elena," Aiden laughs. "Why ever not? You were so eager to be my queen once upon a time."

The look of hurt on Will's face when Aiden says those words is more than I can bear. My adrenaline kicks into overdrive, aided by the anger mixing with the other emotions pounding through my body. The combination numbs the pain in my head long enough to allow me to struggle. I manage to flip over to my knees and grab his ankle, pulling his foot out from under him. He doesn't fall though; I'm not that lucky. But he does lose his grip on my hair.

I scramble to my feet, looking wildly around for a weapon. Aside from splintered wood from the ship, I see nothing of use. I don't want to lose my chance, though, so I gather every ounce of strength and energy I can and charge at him. Aiden sees me coming and tries to lift himself into the air, out of reach, but I am desperate and fueled by pure adrenaline and hate. Pushing off as hard as I can with my legs, I launch myself at Aiden.

I connect with a thud, wrapping my arms around his bare torso, tackling him out of the air. We crash to the floor, landing amid the rubble. A guttural scream erupts from my lips as I attack Aiden, punching, clawing, choking. He throws me off, and then he's gone, back in the air. My nails left long, deep scratches on his face and neck, and his lip is bleeding, but he seems otherwise unharmed. I can't help but feel a surge of pride that I was able to hurt him, though, to make him bleed. I wonder if Will feels it, too. I hope he does.

"Bad form," Aiden scolds, hovering just feet above me. "You need to be punished."

I don't have enough energy to fight him off anymore—the effort it took to run and tackle him to the deck drained me. Whatever punishment Aiden is planning, it could easily be my death sentence. He's inches away from me now, staring down at me with those incredible green eyes. He reaches out like he might touch my cheek, but then his hand clamps down around my throat instead. He rises into the air, lifting me with impossible strength.

"You know, darling," Aiden croons. "I was going to let our dear Will live and take only your life." He turns me so that I'm looking at Will, who is struggling to get to his feet. A look of sheer terror is plastered on his beautiful face. "But after your little outburst," Aiden continues, his grip on my throat tightening. "Now I am going to kill Will while you watch, and then I am going to kill you."

Aiden whistles, and a dozen balls of light appear, circling Will, closing in on him. I'm gasping for air, starving for oxygen. My vision is beginning to go black at the edges. I try to call out to Will, to tell him that I'm sorry, that I can't fight anymore, that I'm not strong enough. I try to tell him that I love him, but nothing comes out. The blackness is closing in on me, just as the fairies close in on Will. The last thing I see is his beautiful face, twisted with pain, his clear blue eyes locked onto mine. And then, there is nothing.

The boy hauls Elena over his shoulder once she loses consciousness, a nasty smile on his angelic face. The fairies are doing just as he asked: making his brother suffer for his indiscretions. They claw at him with sharp nails and bite at him with their tiny, sharp teeth. As much as he wishes he could stay on the ship and watch as the life fades from his brother's eyes, he needs to get to the Rock, to complete the ritual.

His magic shudders. Yes, it is time. With a last look at the pirate who was once his brother, Aiden rockets into the air, heading for the island, the girl's weight not even enough to slow him down. After a few moments, Elena's body goes rigid, telling him that she is awake already, that she can see the death and destruction behind him. He smiles and flies faster.

⟡

The captain swats at the fairies buzzing around him like flies. They bite and scratch at him, poke at him with sharpened sticks. He slaps one out of the air in front of his face. It hits the deck with a tiny crunch and stays down. He cringes. He does not enjoy taking life. Unless that life belongs to Aiden. Taking life only feeds the darkness that roils inside of him, makes it stronger. But he will enjoy taking the life of his brother if he gets off this ship alive. He shakes the thoughts from his head. He cannot concern himself with the lives of fairies controlled by the demon who was once his brother.

He stares at the place in the sky where Aiden disappeared with the girl. His girl. His Elena. One of the fairies darts in, swiping at his face with its tiny, sharp nails. He slaps it away, his injured shoulder burning with pain. The screams of his crew, his friends, fill the air, mingling with the splashing and ripping. The Jolly Roger shudders. A loud crack like lightning mixes with the other sounds in the air, followed by the sound of splintering wood and a deep groan as the main mast begins to sway, to tip, to fall.

His ship, his beautiful ship. The ship he himself carved from the ancient trees of the island so many years ago. But there is no time to mourn the loss of his crew, of the Jolly Roger. He must figure out a way to get to the island, to save the girl he loves more than his own life. He cringes, not at the pain in his shoulder, but at the thought of her in

Aiden's hands.

Pride swelled in his chest when Elena fought back against the boy. When she tackled him out of the air and began raging against him, he almost burst with it. A smile tugs at his lips. He has no doubt that she will keep fighting until her very last breath. The fire inside her burns much too hot to let her give up. But she will need help if she is to defeat Aiden. She needs his help.

The captain rallies his strength one last time, beating back the swarming fairies with his fists. One by one they drop to the deck, dead or incapacitated, he doesn't really care. The remaining few snarl and advance on him with renewed rage.

Fifteen

For a few blissful seconds after I open my eyes, I feel nothing. No pain, no cold, no heartbreak. For a few seconds, I'm completely numb. Then reality comes crashing down around me. I realize that I'm slung over Aiden's shoulder, flying away from the Jolly Roger. Flying away from Will. *Oh no. Will.* A brief memory flashes through my mind. Fairies closing in on Will, his face marred by pain as they claw and bite at him.

I swear that I can hear my heart breaking as I realize the awful truth. I will never see Will again. He is dead. The ship, engulfed in flames and chaos, is getting farther away. The water around the ship churns white. I catch a brief glimpse of a tail in the water. The mermaids—they came. But it wasn't enough.

They couldn't save the Jolly Roger and its crew from Aiden's wrath. I watch as a mermaid launches out of the sea, snatches a fairy out of the air, rips it in half, and drags it down to the ocean depths. The sound it makes when the mermaid rips the fairy in two sounds like a sheet of paper being torn from a notebook.

I know that I am going to die tonight. Aiden is going to kill me and claim my life as his. My remaining years will keep him young and beautiful, and I will be reduced to bones and dust. I also know that there is nothing that I can do to stop him. There's no one to save me, not anymore. I can't even save myself. The Jolly Roger fades from view, which means we are getting closer to the island, closer to my demise.

It feels like only minutes have passed when Aiden begins circling the island, much like he did the night he brought me here. But more time must have passed than I thought. It took the Jolly Roger days, weeks actually, to get to where we were in the middle of the Never Sea. Aiden doesn't land yet, though. He makes a wide arc and keeps going, toward the strange, shadowy place I saw when we flew in. Even in the dark of night, the smaller island is darker than the rest, shrouded in permanent blackness. *How fitting…*

Aiden lands on a narrow, rocky shore, tossing me onto the ground like a ragdoll. I scramble to my feet, hoping that there could be a chance to escape. But when I stand, I find myself face to face with Aiden. His green eyes are locked onto mine, his dagger at my throat. It's strange, the fact that those eyes used to have such a hold over me. One look into them and I fell easily into a trance, unable to look away or reject anything he said. Now, though, I feel nothing but hate and rage when I look into them. Maybe it's because I know what those eyes hold: secrets and hate and evil. Or maybe it's because another pair of eyes, so alike and yet so different from these, have taken hold of me now.

Something behind Aiden catches my eye. A rock the size of a large house takes up most of the small island. The size isn't what's strange about it, though; it's what it looks like that startles me. It's the exact shape of a human skull, complete with eyes and a gaping mouth, which I assume is the entrance to the inside. I have to get away from this place. I won't die here. Not tonight, not ever.

Glancing around, I see that we are standing on top of a large boulder, the beach to one side, the sea to the other.

"Don't bother, Elena," Aiden sneers. "There's nowhere to run."

That's what he thinks...

Ducking to the side, I take a few running steps and leap off the rock toward the ocean. But before I hit the water, Aiden is there, pulling me back by the collar of my shirt. He throws me down with that inhuman strength. My head hits the rock with a sickening crunch and my vision flickers. He doesn't wait for me to try to get to my feet again.

Instead, he takes me by the arm and drags me down off the rock, onto the sand, toward the skull's mouth. The dark trail stretching behind us in the sand tells me that my head is bleeding, *again*. But I don't care. I'd rather die from blood loss than let him take my remaining years for himself. I will welcome death if it means Aiden is deprived of his long life.

A strange sound fills the air suddenly. It sounds like singing, but the voice is eerie, unnerving. A tiny flutter of hope springs to life in my chest. *Mermaids.* Aiden freezes, which sparks the hope in me a little more. The mermaid's song swirls around us, filling the still, balmy air. Aiden starts moving again, more quickly now, killing the hope I had for one sweet minute. He hustles down the path, still dragging me behind him.

My shoulder and my head are screaming with pain. It's almost too much. But I have a feeling that the pain is the only thing keeping me conscious. I can tell by the fuzziness of my vision that I probably have a concussion from the multiple blows to the head. I feel cold despite the warm night. I've lost a lot of blood too, then.

By the time Aiden drags me inside the mouth of the skull rock, I can't feel my feet, or the arm he drags me by. The mermaid's song fades more and more the farther we get from the sea, and now, inside the cave, it's gone completely. My hope along with it. Finally, Aiden drops my arm, leaving me lying on the sand. Inside the skull rock, it is completely silent. I manage to roll over onto my stomach and look around the inside of the rock.

I see that it's not just a rock, but a great cave. The floor of the cave is sand, like the beach and the path. I can feel it stuck to the back of my clothes, in my hair matted with blood, in my eyes, my nose. But only the ground is sand. Everything else inside the cave is rock: the walls, the domed ceiling—all rock. The most disturbing thing about the cave is the large, raised rock slab in the middle of the room. It looks like a table, or an altar. A circle of candles around the altar provides the only light. The dancing flames cast long shadows on the pale rock walls.

I try to push myself to my feet, but can't. I'm too weak. All I can do is drag myself through the sand, centimeter by centimeter, inch by inch, back toward the mouth of the cave. If I can just make it out, if I can just make it to the water, maybe the mermaids can save me. They must have followed us here, and by Aiden's reaction when he heard their song, they probably aren't here to help him kill me.

Risking a quick glance back over my shoulder, I see that Aiden is standing in front of the rock slab, his back turned on me, his arms held out to the side, palms facing up. I use all my remaining strength to drag myself as fast as I can, which isn't very fast. I'm almost to the mouth of the cave now, and hope surges inside me. Just a few more feet and I'll be out. But Aiden stops me again, takes hold of my hair, yanks my head back, and holds his beautiful, jeweled, wickedly sharp dagger to my throat. I can feel the cold metal biting into my skin.

"Do not do that again," Aiden hisses into my ear.

Hauling me to my feet, he half pushes, half drags me to the stone altar in the center of the cave. His hand is still fisted in my hair, and my scalp screams with pain. I find myself wondering if I'll have any hair left when this is over. Not that it will matter when I'm dead. I can feel blood dripping down my face and the back of my neck from my head injuries.

I want to fight back, to dig my feet into the sand, kick, scream, rage against Aiden. But I'm afraid. I know that if I don't fight, I will die. But I'm still afraid. I don't want the end to come sooner than it has to. If I fight, his dagger could easily cut my throat, and then it would be over. I don't want it to be over. Aiden shoves me onto the slab, his dagger still trained on me, but no longer against the delicate skin of my throat.

"I must admit, Elena," he smiles down at me. "You have put up an admirable fight. But I am tired of playing now."

All I can do is look up at him through tear-blurred eyes and beg the universe to save me.

"Do you know what is going to happen now, darling?" Aiden asks.

I can tell by the tone of his voice that he's enjoying this. It makes me sick. "You're going to kill me," I say, my voice dull, flat, devoid of all emotion. I can't believe I ever thought that he was beautiful and good. I can't believe that I came to this world for him. I came here because I wanted to be his queen… *Pathetic.* The only good thing that came from me coming to Neverland was meeting Will. And he's gone now.

"Yes," Aiden sneers, his voice full of malice, laced with honey. "I am going to kill you. But not to worry, I will make it quick."

He runs his thumb along the blade of the dagger, the jewels in its hilt catching the candlelight and sparkling beautifully. This beautiful, dangerous thing will end my life. Beautiful and evil, just like Aiden. The strange, simple crown he wears on his head catches my eye. The stones in it are pulsing. Light, dark, light, dark. In the back of my mind, I wonder if there is a connection between the crown and Aiden's immense power.

I close my eyes. No point in dwelling on something that I have no power to stop. I'm no match for Aiden. And I may have accepted my fate, but that doesn't mean that I have to watch it happen.

"Goodbye, Elena," he whispers.

I squeeze my eyes shut even tighter, waiting for the end to come. But it doesn't. Instead, there's a crash. The thud of a body hitting the sand, the clang of metal hitting stone.

My eyes fly open. Aiden is no longer standing over me. He's nowhere in sight. I can hear scuffling beyond my line of vision and sit up, regretting it instantly. My head spins and nausea washes over me, but I push through it. I look behind me, my body screaming as I twist to do so. In the shadows at the edge of the room, two figures are on the ground, rolling in the sand, fighting. One of the figures is Aiden. Even in the shadows I can see the flash of his golden-brown hair. The other figure seems familiar as well, but while Aiden is light, the other is dark and the shadows swallow him.

The way he moves though… it's so familiar. I'd know him anywhere. *Will.*

The boy can hardly contain his excitement. The time has finally come. His magic will be fully restored, and the aging will stop once again. A shudder ripples through his body as his magic gutters for what will be the last time, for a few years at least. He turns away from the altar to retrieve the girl he left bleeding out in the sand, but miraculously, she has managed to drag herself almost to the cave's entrance.

Aiden stalks over, dagger in hand, and yanks her head back by her hair. He puts his stunning blade to her soft throat and hauls her up from the sand.

"Do not do that again," he hisses in her ear before shoving her toward the stone slab. Aiden pushes her down until she is stretched out on the stone, waiting for what he is going to do to her. He keeps the dagger trained on her, in case she should get it in her head to try something extremely stupid.

He looks down at the girl, his queen, Elena, with her hazel eyes full of tears and despair, and he smiles. "I must admit, Elena, you have put up an admirable fight. But I am tired of playing now," he sneers. She says nothing, only stares up at him, tears streaming from her eyes.

"Do you know what is going to happen now, darling?" he asks, the joy and excitement thrumming through his veins with each beat of his immortal heart.

"You're going to kill me," she replies, her voice flat.

He frowns slightly. "Yes. I am going to kill you. But not to worry, I will make it quick," he says, running his thumb along the wicked sharp blade of his dagger.

She doesn't answer his taunt, and anger boils inside him. It is much less fun when his prey has given up, when they don't fight back any longer.

Aiden lifts his prized dagger over his head and smiles down at the beautiful girl whose blood will give him life. "Goodbye, Elena."

He watches as she squeezes her eyes shut, waiting for her death, and he smiles broadly. But just as he brings the dagger down, right over her heart, he is knocked off his feet.

The pirate hauls himself onto the rocky shore of the small island, shivering and in quite a lot of pain. He waves his thanks to the frightening creatures who brought him here to save the woman he loves. The mermaids' song fades as they sink back to the ocean depths.

His heart had almost stopped when he felt them brush against his legs after he fled his ship, after he dove into the roiling ocean to escape the biting, clawing fairies. When he saw the sharp teeth and glimmer-

ing tails, though, hope filled his heart. He enlisted the help of the beasts who had indeed come to his aid, and let them carry him across the sea, to the small island that is home to Aiden's favorite place, Skull Rock.

Breathing hard, the pirate rushes toward the mouth of the cave. He knows all too well what goes on in that cave, the unspeakable things Aiden does to beautiful young girls inside. Faster, he must run faster. His knees wobble as he approaches the cave's entrance, and he stops just inside the mouth, in the small space between it and the main chamber, and braces himself against the cool stone.

Then he hears her, his Elena. And Aiden's voice as well, taunting her. It turns his stomach. And then he is moving again, rushing to save the only girl he has ever truly felt for. He comes to a halt when he sees Elena lying on the stone slab, Aiden's sacrificial altar. The demon boy who used to be his brother has his back to the entrance, his jeweled dagger raised over his head, ready to plunge it into her heart.

"Goodbye, darling," Aiden says softly.

The pirate remains frozen in place for a second too long before his legs start working again. He charges at the boy, knocking him to the ground, his shoulder burning with pain.

SIXTEEN

Fighting against the pain and fuzziness in my head, I scramble off the stone slab. The sand muffles the thud my body makes when I hit the ground on my hands and knees. The impact, though it wasn't rough, still sends my head spinning. I struggle to focus on the sound of the fighting.

I have to help Will. He survived; he came for me. And now I need to help him. Pushing myself to my feet, I stumble toward the fighting men. What I'm going to do to help… *that* I don't know yet. I'm just kind of winging it at this point, but I'm lucky to even be alive. I'm a little concerned though. If I can't think clearly, anything I try to do might hurt, not help.

Aiden has Will pinned against the wall now, trying to get his jeweled dagger to his throat. Will is fighting back, though. He has dropped his own dagger, but the hook that replaces his left hand is dug deep into Aiden's shoulder. A thin red line of blood trickles down his bare, muscular back. Scanning the ground quickly, I catch a glimpse of Will's dagger, lying half buried in the sand. I don't feel very confident that I'll be able to get to it without being seen, but I have to try.

Quickly, I formulate a rough plan in my head. Instead of going directly for the dagger, I need to create a diversion that will free Will; then he can finish the job while I'm keeping Aiden occupied. It sounds like a great plan in my head, but the execution is what will be difficult.

I take a few shaky steps forward, then quicken my pace until I'm running right at Aiden. Each step causes my head to throb dangerously, but I push through. I jump onto Aiden's back, but my aim is a little off. I hit him with the full force of my body, grab him by the shoulders, and pull him to the ground. His body lands on top of mine, knocking the breath from my lungs with a *whoosh*.

When I dragged Aiden down, Will's hook was ripped from his shoulder, leaving a large, open gash. Blood drips down onto my face as Aiden looms above me. I shove him off, roll onto my stomach, and begin groping the sand, hoping to find Will's dagger. Just as my hand closes around cool metal, Aiden pulls me up, flips me over, and slams me to the ground.

The boy smiles as he slams his brother into the stone wall of the cave. He knows that he is so clever and so fierce, such a skilled fighter. He does not doubt that he will win this fight and put his brother down for good. The pirate will never interfere with his plans again. Aiden roars as the pirate buries his gleaming hook into his shoulder.

He slams Will into the stone again and again, but his brother does not lose consciousness, does not back down from the fight. The boy drives his dagger up, angled for the pirate's throat, but Will takes hold of his arm, forcing his hand down, the dagger getting farther from its target.

The pirate watches Elena over Aiden's shoulder. He watches as she rolls off the altar, as she pushes herself to her feet. He can see the pain etched across her features, the disorientation in her eyes. She sways on her feet, watching the fight.

The pirate struggles to keep the beautiful, wicked dagger away from his throat. He must keep Aiden busy, keep his attention off of Elena so that she can escape. The mermaids will get her away from this cursed island, away from the demon boy.

Something—determination, maybe—flashes across her face. The pirate's stomach drops into his feet when he realizes what she is about to do.

Out of nowhere, the boy is hit from behind with enough force to knock him to the ground. During the fall, his brother's hook tears through his shoulder, leaving a gaping, gushing wound. He lands on top of a soft body, and as his vision clears, he realizes that it is his queen, Elena. The blood flowing from his shoulder drips onto her dirty face, mixing with her own.

She pushes him off of her and begins scrambling away, her hands raking through the sand—searching for something, he realizes. Rage boils inside of him. The boy has grown very, very tired of the girl's antics. He grabs her by the back of her filthy shirt, flips her over, and slams her into the sand with all his strength.

Will roars with anger and launches himself at Aiden, trying to pull him off of me, but Aiden pushes him back with that inhuman strength he somehow possesses. My hand, still outstretched, searches the sand, closing around the dagger's hilt just as Aiden turns back to me.

"You know," he hisses, his face hovering inches above mine. "I found your fire appealing at first. It made you interesting. But now, I find it irritating and tiresome."

"Well, I'm not exactly a fan of yours anymore either," I say, squirming beneath his weight. Aiden's face goes red with anger.

He rears back and slaps me hard across the face. "How dare you mock me!" he roars.

A smile spreads slowly across my face, even as I taste the coppery tang of the blood leaking into my mouth from my now split lip. When Aiden slapped me, he released my arm, leaving the hand that is holding the dagger now free. More quickly than I imagined I could move, I bring my arm up, burying the dagger into Aiden's side. His eyes go wide with… Fear? Pain? Shock? Maybe all three. But it is so satisfying. Blood gushes out of the wound, coating my hand and the hilt of the dagger with hot, sticky blood.

Aiden's eyes, still wide, start to glaze over. He opens his mouth, but no sound comes out. I watch the light go out of his eyes, leaving the once stunning green gaze cold and blank. Like two lifeless, pale green stones. Like the strange green stones in the crown now lying half buried in the sand. He collapses on top of me, and the air is forced from my lungs again. But I feel glorious.

The boy slaps Elena hard across the face, her bottom lip splitting open.

"How dare you mock me!" he roars as the rage threatens to boil over. He must not kill her, though, not yet. The ritual isn't complete. But it does not mean that he cannot enjoy every second of her demise.

Her face breaks into a smile, smug and full of venom. Confusion flashes through his mind just before she drives her hand up and searing pain races through every inch of his body. He looks to where the worn hilt of a dagger protrudes form his side, ruby blood gushing out around it, coating the girl's pale hand, sliding down his ribs, darkening the sand.

The boy opens his mouth to say… what? He cannot form any words, not while the magic and blood drains from his body. He looks into the girl's hazel eyes, and for just a moment, he feels something that he has not felt for many years. Regret. Then his vision darkens, and he knows that his time has come.

⟡

The pirate struggles to his feet, his body aching from head to toe. He starts for the pair again. If Elena dies for him… well, he does not know what he will do. He is out of weapons and his strength is failing, but he must help her. He must save her.

The darkness inside of him surges, wanting to spill blood, to kill. Then Aiden slaps Elena across the face, hard. Her head snaps to the side so he can see her face clearly, but her eyes are unfocused, half glazed with pain and fear and rage. Blood trickles from the lip his brother just split open with his hand. But then… something strange happens.

A smile spreads lazily across her bleeding, bruised, dirty face. The pirate cannot fathom why she would be smiling. Time seems to stop for a long minute. Then he sees her arm go up, the dagger he dropped clutched in her hand. Elena buries the blade as deep as it will go into Aiden's side, somehow slipping it between his ribs without even aiming.

Blood gushes, coating the hilt of the dagger, her hand, her arm, the pale sand turning red. The pirate feels his mouth drop open with shock, and then a smile much like Elena's stretches across his face. Pride swells inside his chest, shoving the darkness down deep. Will rushes to Elena's aid, but stops a few steps short at the sight of the lifeless body lying on top of hers.

And just for a moment, the pirate wishes that he could have somehow saved his brother from this fate.

It's over. I did it. I killed Aiden. Will is alive, and Aiden is dead. And then Will is there, hauling Aiden's lifeless body off me. He drops the corpse on the ground and pulls me to my feet, into his arms, his lips finding mine, and the stars align. Tears spill down my cheeks, but for the first time in a long time, they aren't sad tears, but tears of joy.

"You're alive!" I gasp when he breaks the kiss. "I thought you were dead! I thought I'd lost you!"

"Oh, Elena," Will murmurs against my mouth. "To die would be an awfully big adventure. And I'm not quite done with this one yet."

A sob escapes past my lips, and then his mouth is on mine again. He kisses me deeply, hungrily, until all the pain, all the fear, all the bad things that have happened all disappear. He kisses me until all that's left in the world is the two of us.

Seventeen

We leave Aiden's body in the cave. It seems like a fitting spot for his final resting place. Will keeps a tight hold on my hand as we walk out into the coming night. Outside, a few fairies hover in the air, a good distance away from the giant skull rock. I recoil at the sight of the familiar balls of light, remembering the last time I saw them, when they were closing in on the man by my side.

Will pushes me behind him, shielding me with his body. For a few long seconds, the fairies just hover, watching us from within their glow. Then there's a flash, and the fairies have changed. They are in their larger form now, more human-like, though their human form is still quite a bit smaller than a regular person.

"What do you want?" Will growls at them.

The fairy at the front of the group holds up her hands. It takes me a moment, but I realize that it's Tatiana.

"We are not here to fight, pirate," she says. Her eyes slide to me, peeking out around Will's shoulder. "Elena." She nods, her green eyes sparkling in the darkness.

"Tatiana," I say coolly.

Tatiana looks back to Will and says, "We mean you no harm."

Will snorts. "So what were you trying to do when you attacked my ship and killed my crew?"

The fairy blanches but narrows her eyes. "We did not want to attack you, William," she says through clenched teeth. "Aiden controlled us, much like he controlled the weather and the island itself. He compelled us to do many things we did not want to do," she finishes, the sparkle in her eyes disappearing.

I think immediately of Aiden's bright, strange eyes, how they captivated me every time he looked at me, how I melted and forgot all my worries, how I did exactly as he wanted. Was he controlling me, too? A shiver slides down my spine. He must have been controlling me. It is the only reasonable explanation I can think of for some of my actions.

Will regards the fairies, who are blocking our path off the small island, but he doesn't reply. Instead, it's me who speaks next.

"Tatiana, you say Aiden controlled you all, but he is dead now," I say.

She nods. "I felt the connection break when his light went out."

I step out from behind Will, not afraid of the fairies who stand incredibly still in front of us. "If your connection to Aiden is broken, and you aren't here to harm us... then why are you here?" I ask.

Tatiana smiles sadly. "To make up for the trouble we have

caused. To see if there is something we can do to redeem our-selves," she says, glancing back and forth between our faces.

I hear the growl rumble in Will's chest and lace my fingers through his, squeezing lightly. "I can think of a few things that you can do for us," I muse, wincing at the pain still pounding through my body with each heartbeat.

Tatiana's bright eyes spark when she sees the wince, then travel over my body and Will's, taking in our various wounds and injuries.

"I can heal those for you, if you would like." She nods at the spot where blood still leaks from his shoulder, and my head.

"That would be a start," Will snaps.

The fairy's eyes land on him again. "I wish that I could bring your crew back, Captain," she murmurs. "I wish that it was in my power, but as you know, I cannot bring back the dead."

Will stiffens beside me. I squeeze his hand a little tighter. "Can you repair the Jolly Roger with your magic?" he asks.

She smiles faintly and dips her head in a nod.

"Can you take me home?" I ask without really deciding to speak at all, especially to ask that question. I feel when every muscle in his body goes rigid. I told him once that this was my home now, that he was my home, and I meant it. But . . .

Tatiana smiles faintly. "Yes, Elena. I can take you home if that is what you wish."

I feel Will's eyes on me, but I can't make myself look at him. The hurt and the rage radiating from his body breaks my heart just a bit, adding to the cracks and holes already there. My mouth opens, then closes as I contemplate my next words very, very carefully. "Maybe," I finally say.

Beside me, Will relaxes slightly, but the tension in his body is still obvious. "I'd like to have my things from Aiden's tree-house," I say, thinking of the bag of belongings that were left there when Will rescued me from Aiden's clutches. The fairy nods and snaps her fingers, and my bag appears at my feet, the blanket and my clothes stuffed inside. "Thank you," I say softly.

The fairy snaps her fingers again, looks to Will, and says, "Your ship is whole again, waiting for you where you left it. And any of your crew still alive have been healed of their injuries as well."

"Thank you," he says, his voice tight.

"Anything else?" the fairy asks.

"Can you get us back to the ship?" I ask.

Tatiana snaps her fingers, and then we are back on the deck of the Jolly Roger.

The ship is completely restored to its former glory—no sign of the destruction and death anywhere to be found. A handful of the remaining crew are there, waiting on the deck for the return of their captain. Will drops my hand like it's on fire and stalks to his crew, clapping them all on the back. I hang back, not sure what to do now. He is clearly angry with me, and hurt, and doesn't want me around, but… I have nowhere else to go. Unless I go home.

The thought of going back to London, back to that rundown school, turns my stomach. Would Will come back with me if I return? Or will he choose to let me go, to stay with his ship and his men?

"Elena." His voice breaks me out of my thoughts. "Join me in my quarters please. I'm having a bath drawn for you."

My heart flutters at the thought of being alone with him again, for the first time since our fight the night before Aiden's attack.

I pick up my bag and walk slowly across the deck, toward the beautiful man I love, toward the room that we have shared for weeks. My heartrate picks up, anticipating what is to come. Or what I hope is going to happen. Will holds the door to the cabin open for me and closes it behind us. The room is dark, and my eyes strain to watch him stride around the room, lighting the oil lamps. He doesn't speak, and neither do I.

A knock at the door makes me jump. Will crosses the room, opens it, and lets his massive first mate haul in the copper tub and fill it with hot water. When the pirate leaves, Will closes the door again and grabs a stack of fresh towels before sauntering over to where I'm standing, his blue eyes locked onto mine. He doesn't look away as he dips the corner of a towel into the water and begins to wash the blood off my face.

"Please say something," I whisper.

His mouth thins, and his eyes harden. "What would you like me to say?" he asks.

I shrug. He sighs, handing me the towel and stripping off his ruined shirt. Apparently, it's my turn to wash the blood off of him. Dipping the towel into the water, I set to work, cleaning the blood from his chest where a gaping wound once was in his shoulder. He turns, letting me clean his back.

"I'm sorry," I say finally. "I don't know why I asked that question. I don't want to leave you, Will."

He turns to face me, taking the towel from me and dropping it to the floor. His bright eyes bore into mine with such intensity that I have to force myself not to look away.

"Then do not leave." The words are barely a whisper. My breath catches in my throat. "I love you, Elena," he says, his voice still hushed. "I do not ever want to be without you. Not even for a minute, not even for a second."

"Will…" I try to say, but he cuts me off.

"I know you are still young, and I know that I look young, but I have been alive for a very, very long time. In all that time, I have never met anyone like you. I have never felt for anyone like I feel for you. I want you to stay so that I can make you the happiest girl that has ever lived."

My vision goes blurry with tears. When one slips down my

cheek, he quickly wipes it away with his thumb.

"Don't cry, love. Just tell me that you will stay with me," he pleads.

"Will, I love you. I know I'm young and most people would say that I don't know what real love is, but that's crap, because I *love* you. There's this… *pull,* toward you. I've felt it since the minute I opened my eyes and looked up into your face the night you rescued me," I say, putting my hands on his muscular chest.

"Then stay," he whispers, his own eyes filling with tears.

"Would you consider coming back with me? To my world?" I ask.

His eyes go wide, then crinkle at the edges as he laughs softly, "I'm not sure a one-handed pirate would fit in in your world, love."

My heart plummets into my stomach. "I don't know if I can stay here. Not after all that's happened," I say, forcing my eyes to look away from his.

He nods his understanding, but the tears in his eyes begin to overflow and he turns away, bracing his hands on the desk.

"Will, don't shut me out. *Please.*" I take a couple steps and put my hand on his back, but he shrugs it off and walks away. He pulls a fresh shirt from a drawer, pulls it on and sweeps past me without looking at me.

"You should bathe, before the water gets cold," he says before he walks out of the room, slamming the heavy door behind him with a bang. I put my face in my hands, the tears flowing freely, sliding between my fingers and falling to the floor.

The pirate slams the heavy door behind him. He knew this day would come. He had hoped that it would not, but it was a foolish hope. Of course, Elena wanted to return to her own world. Neverland is no place for a girl like her. She is smart and cunning and beautiful. She deserves to be around people, make friends, and start a family one day, in a place where she can thrive.

He can feel his heart breaking with each step he takes across the deck of the Jolly Roger, spider web cracks spreading from the center, where he has held Elena since the day he brought her onto this ship. Reaching the bow, Will braces his hands on the wooden rail and closes his eyes.

The darkness that has plagued him for many years begins to rise, threatening to engulf his heart, his mind. The pirate has spent so long trying to keep the dark at bay, to prevent it from taking control of him. But now… Elena is going to leave him. She is going to leave him in the claws of that darkness, and it will consume him once and for all.

I take my time bathing and dressing. The longer I take, the longer Will has to cool down some, and the longer I have to think about the decision that I know I have to make. To leave or not to leave, that is the question… A question I can't answer. A question I might never be able to answer. But I have to figure out what I want on my own.

Dipping my head under the warm water, I massage my scalp carefully at first, then harder when I realize that the injuries are not even tender, the wounds now fully healed thanks to Tatiana's magic. The water in the tub quickly turns a murky shade of pink from the blood and the sand and the sweat that coats most of my body.

I linger in the tub even after I'm clean. Pulling my legs to my chest, I wrap my arms around them, resting my chin on my knees. The events of the last twenty-four hours run on a loop through my mind. My fight with Will, Aiden's attack on the ship, Skull Rock. A shudder rips through my body when Aiden's dying face flashes behind my closed eyelids. The way the light left his eyes, the way the blood gushed out from between his ribs, coating my hand. The reality of the situation hits me like a truck.

Aiden is dead. I killed him. I *murdered* someone today. Does that make me as bad as Aiden? It was in self-defense; it wasn't like I wanted to kill him. It was necessary for my survival, for Will's survival. But… a ball of ice forms in the pit of my stomach nonetheless. I *killed* someone today. How can I go back to my own world, just go to school and go on with my life like it never happened?

I don't think that I can do that. But I don't think that I can stay here either. Stepping foot on the island will be so hard. Seeing the fairy tree, the lake, and the ruined waterfall, knowing that Skull Rock is shrouded by shadows in the distance, just out of sight. I can't imagine spending an eternity here. Because if I do stay here, it will be forever, because even though Aiden is dead, Neverland's magic lives on. If I stay here, I will never age. I will be seventeen forever.

Of course, there are other things to consider when making my decision. Like Will. How can I leave him? How can I leave the love of my life behind and pretend that we never happened? I can't help but think that if I leave Neverland, I will never find someone who fills the Will-sized hole in my heart.

The water is cold by now, and my body is trembling—from the cold or from the shock of what I've done, I'm not sure. Hastily, I climb from the tub, wrapping a towel around myself. I cross the room to where my bag is now lying on the bed, the bed that I have shared with Will for many nights, the bed where I gave myself to him—to anyone—for the first time. I shake my head as if it will knock the thoughts from my head, grab the bag, and turn away, fresh tears burning in my eyes.

I carry the bag over to the massive desk, careful to keep my back to the bed, and dig for the spare clothes I brought. Pulling on the leggings and sweater, I revel at the softness of my own clothes compared to the rough shirts and pants I've been borrowing from the crew. Next, I pull out the blanket, my favorite blanket, and bury my nose in it. Somehow, even after the weeks it was held hostage by Aiden, it still smells like lavender and vanilla, still smells like home.

In the time I've been here, I forgot what I packed in the bag that night, the night he came for me, so I stick my hand in the back and grope along the bottom until my hand brushes over the cover of a book. Pulling it out, I turn it over and read the title. *Peter Pan.* My stomach turns, bile rising in my throat.

I was so stupid to think that my time in Neverland would be anything like the story. When Aiden appeared in my dorm room that night, I should have known. I should have been able to see the evil that festered inside of him, rotting his soul. My fingers travel over the worn cover, over the lettering and the cracking spine.

Wrapping the knit blanket around my shoulders, I hold the book against my chest and stalk out of the room. I climb the stairs to the upper deck, careful not to look around for fear of meeting Will's eyes. I keep walking until I reach the railing at the stern, where I drop the blanket to the deck. Taking the book in my hands, I let my eyes and my fingers take it in one last time, and then I throw it into the sea.

Retrieving my blanket, I wrap myself up again and head back to the cabin, keeping my eyes straight ahead, not looking at anyone. Out of the corner of my eye, I see the familiar black hair, catch a flash of icy blue eyes, but I don't look. I can't. Not until I've made my decision on whether to stay or to leave. Instead, I descend the stairs and close myself into the cabin. My body is heavy with exhaustion, so I lay down on the bed, trying my best not to think about what has gone on between the silk sheets. I bury my face in the blanket and let myself fall asleep with something other than the smell of salt and wind in my nose.

The captain watches the girl he loves stalk up the stairs. His heartbeat quickens at the thought that she is coming to him, to tell him that she has changed her mind, that she is going to stay with him in Neverland. His eyes travel over her, taking in her wet hair, her scrubbed face, the grey blanket he has never seen before draped over her shoulders, the strange clothes she is wearing. The smell of lavender and something sweeter floats to him on the breeze.

His eyes bore into her, willing her to look his way, but she does not. Instead, she walks right past him without even a glance. More cracks spread across his heart as he watches her approach the stern. She stops, her back to him, and lets the blanket drop to the deck. It is then that he notices the worn book clutched in her hands. He watches as she runs her fingers over the cover and unceremoniously tosses it into the sea.

She retrieves the blanket from the deck, pulls it around herself, and turns. His muscles tense; he thinks that now she will come to him. But again, she stomps across the deck without so much as a glance in his direction. His eyes follow her down the stairs, where her auburn head disappears around the corner. The pirate hears the door to his quarters open and close again, and he lets out a breath that he did not realize he was holding.

Immediately, the pirate rushes to the stern, where he leans over to locate the book she tossed away. It is there, bobbing in the wake of the moving ship. He locates one of the smaller fishing nets they use for catching meals and casts it into the water, ensnaring the book. The pirate hauls the net and his catch up onto the Jolly Roger and takes the book in his hand. It is soggy, falling apart now, but the words on the cover are still legible. *Peter Pan by J.M Barrie* is scrawled in gold letters across the front.

The pirate's heart jumps into his throat at the same time the darkness inside of him surges. An image of the boy who was once his brother shoves into his mind. The blood flowing around the hilt of the dagger. *So much blood.* The way he collapsed on top of Elena. Grief and regret flood his veins, mixing with his blood. The same blood that flowed through the veins of his brother, the same blood that stained the sand and soiled his clothes only hours ago.

He takes one last look at the deteriorating book, wishing that he had been able to read it before the sea ruined its pages. Wishing that he could have read what was written about his brother, how the rest of the world, those who did not know him, perceived him. A tear slips down his cheek as he tosses the ruined book back to its watery grave. He stares at it until, finally, it slips beneath the surface and disappears forever.

The pirate lingers a while longer, contemplating whether or not he should go to the girl he loves, whether he should push her for an answer or leave her to her thoughts. When he can resist no longer, he turns, heading for his quarters. When he reaches the door, he hesitates, his hand hovering just above the knob. He takes a deep breath, turns the knob, and pushes open the door. The lamps have been turned down low, so much so that he has to let his eyes adjust before crossing the threshold.

The room is silent, and the pirate wonders if he was wrong about Elena coming back here. Then he notices the grey lump curled up in the center of his bed, the fiery hair peeking out from a fold of the blanket. He debates going to her, curling his body around hers and letting sleep take him as well. But instead, he turns and exits the room.

A tendril of darkness slips inside his heart through one of the many cracks just as the door closes behind him.

EIGHTEEN

My dreams are filled with fighting, fire, destruction, and blood. I wake with a start, my heart pounding, a cold sweat slithering down my body, Aiden's dying eyes still fresh in my mind. Immediately, my hand goes to the other side of the bed, searching for the warm body that usually sleeps next to me. But the bed is cold. A pang of sadness, or maybe regret, hits my heart, but I push it down.

It takes a minute, but my breathing slowly evens out, my heartrate returning to normal. I find myself wondering where Will has been all night, if he's still so angry at me that he doesn't want to be anywhere near me. Sitting up in bed, I stretch my arms up over my head. The blanket I've kept wrapped tightly around myself falls, pooling around my hips. I wince at the ache in every single muscle in my body, despite Tatiana having healed all of my injuries.

Sliding to the side of the bed, I swing my legs over the edge. My feet hit the wooden floor without a sound. Padding to the private bathing chamber at the other side of the room, I take a long look at myself in the dirty mirror. My hair is wild, full of tangles from not brushing it after my bath last night. There are dark, bruise-like smudges under my eyes, even though I slept like the dead once I climbed into bed.

It shocks me how different I look from when I arrived in Neverland. The softness in my face is gone, my features older, harder. I guess that's what happens when you get suckered into flying to a magical world where a fairy-tale-character-turned-serial-killer tries to use your life to keep himself young.

Wow, it sounds so strange, so ridiculous—like something from a book. I never in a million years thought something like that would happen to me. But here I am, and it all did happen. And… and I *killed* someone. Aiden's eyes flash through my mind again. I can almost feel the sticky, hot blood on my hand again.

Shaking the thoughts from my head, I see to my needs, drag a brush through my hair, and set off to find myself some breakfast. With a full stomach, I might be able to make the impossible decision a little easier. I wonder again where Will slept last night, if he slept at all. We barely had a chance to talk after the events in the cave last night. I should really find him, check on him. He told me that he hadn't considered Aiden his brother for a long time, but the reality is that his brother died last night. *I killed his brother last night.*

In the galley, I pile food on a plate and slide onto one of the benches, next to Miles—the massive pirate I met my first night on the Jolly Roger, and Will's first mate. He nods a greeting to me before digging into his own breakfast, which he finishes before I've had a chance to take more than three bites. Slowly, the rest of the crew slips out, returning to their duties.

I'm almost finished when I get the feeling that someone is watching me. Turning to the door, I see Will, still in his filthy clothes, standing there, watching me with despair in his eyes. I pat the bench next to me, and his face softens. Will swings his leg over the bench, straddling it so that he can look at me without turning. He doesn't bother with any of the food.

"You should eat," I say. He just shakes his head. "You didn't come to bed last night," I try again. He smiles, but it doesn't reach his eyes.

"You were asleep by the time I got there. I didn't want to disturb you," he says. The sadness in his eyes, his voice, is almost too much for me to bear.

"Will…" I start, but the words fail me.

He takes my hand in his and brings it to his lips, his warm breath brushing across my knuckles as he says, "It's alright, love. You don't have to say anything. I know it is a hard decision to make, and I do not expect you to make it quickly."

My vision blurs, the tears stinging my eyes. "I love you," I say quietly. It's the only thing I can think of, and it's true. I do love him. I love every inch of him, from his inky black hair to his striking blue eyes, all the way down to his scuffed leather boots, and everything in between. Even the gleaming hook that takes the place of his left hand.

"I know," he says softly.

The pirate does not have the heart to ask her to stay for him, to beg her to stay, even though every inch of his body is screaming to say the words. He can only hold her small, soft hand in his, brush his lips over her fingers, and tell her that he understands. Because he does understand. If he were in her position, he would not want to stay in this wretched place either.

*Elena had asked him to come with her, back to her world. But…
How would that work out? What would people say about the man with
a hook for a hand? What would he do while she went off for her schooling? How would he support her? Because in that world, he would
certainly need money. In Neverland, he can feed her, clothe her, give
her a life, however meager it may be.*

*But why would she want that when she can go back, when she can
have the comforts she has grown up with? Why would she want to stay
in this place? The pirate cannot think of any good reasons.*

"I love you," she says quietly, her eyes filled with tears.

*"I know," he replies. And it is because he loves her that he will let
her go when the time comes.*

Will leaves me sitting on the bench in the empty room, with the
excuse of needing to change and freshen up. But I think he just
wanted to avoid me seeing when his own tears started slipping
down his cheeks. How can I possibly leave him? Sure, I've only
known him for a few weeks, but I can't imagine my life without
him in it. I was wrong; the full stomach is not helping me make
my decision any easier.

Rising from the bench, I start wandering the ship, avoiding
Will's cabin and the deck. There's not many places to go, though.
After a few minutes, I find myself in the hold of the ship, where
the supplies are stored. Wooden crates and boxes stacked floor
to ceiling take up most of the space. Rolled-up nets hang from
the ceiling. The dust floating in the air mixed with the salt water lends a musty, unpleasant smell to the space. I sit down on
one of the closed crates, which, according to the sloppy letters
scrawled across the side, is full of cannonballs. The sound of the
sea lapping against the hull is soothing after living for so long
on the water. It's hypnotic, almost.

I close my eyes, letting the hold fade away, diving deep into my own mind to find the answer to the question I wish I had never asked. Because I never should have asked the fairy to take me home. It was stupid and impulsive and… a good question. My heart is screaming to stay, to hold on to Will with everything I have and never let him go, while my head, my stupid head, is snarling to leave this place. To run far, far away and never look back.

So, which one am I supposed to follow? My head? Or my heart? It would be so much easier if he would just agree to come back with me. I understand that it might seem scary to him, that he's worried about how people will look at a one-handed pirate. But with some modern clothes, a prosthetic hand instead of the hook… no one would ever know. Why haven't I said these things to him? Why am I sulking down here in the dark, avoiding the man that I love?

Stop being such a coward, Elena, I tell myself. But still… I can't make myself get up. Can't make my feet move. Instead, I stay in the dark hold of the ship, my heart and my head at war with each other, until finally, my decision has been made.

Nineteen

I make my way out of the hold and up to the quarterdeck, re-hearsing the words I'm going to say over and over in my head. My feet seem to grow heavier with each step, like someone is slowly filling my boots with lead. It feels like hours before I finally emerge into the sunlight.

Will is exactly where I thought he would be, hand and hook braced on the wheel. His eyes land on me instantly, and his face hardens, as if he knows exactly what I'm about to do. Maybe he does. Maybe my face has the words written all over it.

He drags his bright eyes from my face, choosing to gaze out across the sea instead.

"You've made your decision, then?" he asks, his voice

clipped.

I open my mouth, but no words come out. The speech I spent the past hour preparing has flown right out of my head. So, I just nod.

"You're leaving," he says. A statement, not a question. He still won't look at me.

"Come with me," I plead. I can hear the whine in my voice, but I don't care. He needs to hear the emotion that is burning me up from the inside out. Needs to feel the pain that I'm feeling at having to leave. "Please, Will. Please come with me." *Please, please, please*, I beg silently. The silence that follows my pleas is deafening. More deafening than Aiden's fireball, more than the destruction of the *Jolly Roger. Please.*

Finally, Will turns his head to look at me. His eyes are as hard as the ice that has formed around my heart and in the pit of my stomach. He stares at me without speaking for the longest minute of my life. I shift my weight from foot to foot, clenching and unclenching my fists, willing him to say yes, willing him to say *anything*.

"No," he says, his voice thick with rage and danger.

My heart stops beating, my blood turning to ice in my veins. "No?" I ask. I can feel the color drain from my face, feel my eyes go wide with shock and hurt.

"No," he repeats, not an ounce of emotion showing on his own face. "That world is no place for a pirate with a hook for a hand."

Now the ice is spreading, to my limbs, to my brain. "Will, with all of the modern technology, and with some new clothes, no one would ever know. Please," I beg again.

But he just turns away, his eyes again on the sea, on his ship, and says, "No."

"Oh," I say, my voice barely audible over the sounds of the sea and the ship. Will doesn't say anything else, doesn't look at me. I try to make my feet move, to walk away from the man

I love more than myself, from the man who just shattered my heart into a million tiny pieces, but my legs aren't responding to the commands from my brain, no matter how loud it screams them. All I can do is stand anchored to this spot on the deck and stare at the person who I never thought would hurt me.

I don't know how long I stand there before my feet start working again. Minutes, hours, days, maybe. Will never says another word to me, never looks my way. Somehow, though, I end up back in that dark corner of the hold, the only place I can go for privacy without the chance of *him* coming in. The pain that now coats every sliver of my broken heart is spreading, inching through my veins with every beat of my heart.

How can he treat me like that? Like I'm nothing? I wonder, perching on top of the crate and pulling my knees tight to my chest. I can't even say his name, can't even think it. It hurts too much. We were supposed to be together. We loved each other. Right? But what if it wasn't real? What I felt was real; I have no doubt about that. But what if it was all an act for him? Is it possible that he is that good of an actor? Good enough to fool me for weeks, to make me think he loved me?

The pain spreads again, reaching all the way into my toes, my fingertips, until it is too much to bear. My body, my brain, are screaming in agony, screaming for me to rid them of the horrific sensation. I comply. I allow myself to go numb, let the feeling of nothing spread along the same path the pain took, until I feel absolutely nothing.

⸺❖⸺

The pirate struggles not to look at her face, so full of pain. He forces himself to look at the sea, at the ship he built with his own hands so very long ago. His heart cracks even more with every "please" that passes her lips. The captain wants to go with her, wants to tell her that he will follow her to the ends of the universe and beyond. But he cannot make his mouth speak the words.

The darkness rises up, filling in the cracks spreading along his heart with a blackness so thick, not even her fire can penetrate it; not even her fire can burn it away. It surges again, fighting to take over, to get out. And then, without the permission of his mind, his head turns, and the pirate finds himself looking into those eyes, her eyes. What he sees in them breaks a piece of his heart off, and darkness rushes in to fill the hole.

"No," the darkness makes him say. He tries to fight it, but it is too strong, has too much of a hold over him now.

"No?" she repeats, her face going as white as a sheet, her eyes wide.

"No," the darkness says again. "That world is no place for a pirate with a hook for a hand." The pirate stands, muted by the darkness, while the girl he loves more than himself begs him again to come with her, tells him of all the things they can do so that no one will know what he is. When she finishes, he opens his mouth, hoping to beat the darkness to an answer, but all that comes out is "No."

Elena stands as if frozen in place for a long time. She does not speak, does not so much as flinch. His eyes remain trained on the water surrounding them, on the crew scurrying about on the deck below. Eventually, she turns and wanders below deck.

The pirate wants so badly to run after her, to take her in his arms and tell her he didn't mean any of it, that he loves her and that he will follow her anywhere. But the darkness taking root in his heart is too strong. So here he stands, frozen at the wheel of his ship, while the girl he loves is somewhere on board, losing faith in him, hating him, falling out of love with him.

My eyes open, and I don't know where I am at first. I'm in a small room that smells of dust and dried meat and salty air, sitting on a hard, wooden box. The room is so dark that I can only make out the vague shapes of more boxes stacked throughout the room. *The hold.* I'm still in the hold. Slowly, the events of the day rise to the surface of my thoughts.

"No," he said. More than once, with no doubt in his voice, with no hesitation. *No.*

The pain begins creeping through my veins again, pushing out the numbness that allowed my brain to shut down for a while. Long enough for the sky to darken. *I have to get out of here,* I think. Standing and stretching my stiff limbs, I pick my way across the room, heading for the door. *I have to get out of here.* If I can make it back to the captain's quarters unnoticed, I can grab my things and figure out how to find Tatiana. All I have to do is avoid…

My foot gets tangled in one of the nets strewn about the hold and I go down, hard, my ankle wrenching painfully. The rough floor scrapes my palms when I catch myself to save my face from meeting the unforgiving wood. Instead of untangling my boot, I stay on the floor, curled around myself, the tears flowing freely.

Suddenly, there's a flash that lights up every corner of the room, illuminates every box, every speck of dust floating through the air.

"Hello, Elena," a silvery voice says. *Tatiana.* Slowly, I push myself up, turning to meet those striking green eyes.

"Get me out of here," I beg, too far into the downward spiral of my own heartbreak to even be embarrassed at the pathetic whine in my voice.

Tatiana nods. She doesn't ask if I'm sure, doesn't give me an opportunity to change my mind, to second guess myself. The fairy snaps her fingers; there's another flash, and then I'm hovering above the Jolly Roger, looking down at the quiet, almost deserted deck. Tatiana appears next to me, my bag of belongings in one hand.

"Are you ready?" she asks, her eyes bright, glittering. A

movement on the quarterdeck catches my attention. I know what it is—no, *who* it is—before I even look. And yet, I look anyway.

Will is pacing the deck, his hands behind his back, his eyes on his feet. I watch as he reaches the railing, spins on the heel of his shiny black boot, and paces to the other rail. Rail, spin, pace, repeat. Over and over. Every piece of my shattered heart aches at the sight of him, urges me to change my mind, to go to him. *No,* I tell it. *He made his choice. He made his feelings entirely clear.*

"Elena, are you ready?" The fairy asks again.

I take one last look down at the ship, at the man that I fell for so quickly, so foolishly, then turn to the little blonde fairy beside me. "Yes," I say, willing as much confidence into the word as I can muster.

She nods. "Do you remember the way?"

This time it's me who nods. "Second star to the right?"

"And straight on 'til morning," she smiles, her green eyes crinkling at the corners.

⚜

The pirate paces the deck of his ship. To one side, then the other, then back again, over and over. He hopes that if he keeps moving, maybe his steps will stomp the darkness back down. It has steadily been rising, taking control of him bit by bit. If he lets it take over, there is no telling what kind of heinous things he will do.

The way that he spoke to Elena, the way that he treated her, was despicable. The pirate did not want to say those things, did not want to hurt her, treat her like the fish innards that stain the wooden deck. She came to him out of love, to beg him to go with her, to have a real life with her, and instead of telling her that he loved her, that he wanted nothing more than to live an ordinary life with her, he shut her out.

As he paces, he thinks of how to make it up to her, how to make her forgive him, how to rid himself of the darkness for good. He can feel it inside of him, surging and fighting back, trying to slip tendrils of itself through the cracks in his damaged heart, to snuff out all the light left inside of him. The pirate sees a flash of light out of the corner of his eye. He looks up, but the sky is empty save for the glittering stars. Maybe he imagined it. But the only thing he knows of that flashes like that are… fairies.

It takes a moment for Will's brain to make the connection, but when he does… his steps pound against the deck, echoing through the hold below. He rushes to his quarters and throws open the door, but the room is empty. He turns to go, but something tugs at the edge of his mind. Will steps into the room, turning slowly in a circle, trying to figure out what seems different.

Then it hits him. All of her things are gone. Every piece of clothing, the blanket she cocooned herself in the night she killed his brother, is gone. Her bag that the fairy retrieved from the island is gone. Elena is gone. No, he prays. No, no, no. Please let her be here somewhere. He tears through the ship like a hurricane, looking in every room, every hold, every dark and dusty inch of the Jolly Roger. But she is gone. Elena is gone.

TWENTY

Tatiana leads me up, up, up, away from the island and the Jolly Roger and Neverland… and *him*. Her white-blonde hair shines bright, like a beacon in the dark. We go higher and higher, toward the burning stars that are growing larger every second. After so long on the ship, the sensation of flying is incredible. It's like I'm experiencing it for the first time all over again.

Higher and higher she leads me, picking up speed the closer to the stars we get. The cold wind roars in my ears as it rushes by. The fairy looks over her shoulder at me, a small smile on her face. I try to smile back, to enjoy the feeling of being weightless, of being so close to the celestial beauty, but Will's face won't leave my mind.

Every time I think of the things he said to me, every time I think of how he wouldn't even look at me, my heart splinters a little more. I wish he would have just listened, given me a chance to show him that we could be happy, that we could have a good life together in my world. But he didn't. He shut me out and broke my heart.

I shake my head, trying to focus on the burning stars growing closer as we go higher. The swirling colors, the heat, the sheer size of them. I don't want to forget this. I don't want to forget what happened here, what I felt for Will, what I did to Aiden. No, forgetting is not an option. But there's no point in dwelling on wishes and dreams, on things that I can't control, on things that are in the past now.

Our star is getting closer. I can feel the sweat beading on my brow, soaking my shirt. We are so close to it now that the fear of bursting into flame has come back. But then there's a flash, and the heat is gone, replaced by an icy wind. We begin to descend. London stretches out beneath us, the lights of the city glittering like a sea of stars in the dark. Everything is blanketed in fluffy white snow. It looks like a beautiful postcard. I know that I should feel relief, happiness at being back in my own world. But all I feel is empty.

⁂

Tatiana hovers outside the window of the dorm room that was mine when I left London. I tried to tell her that they have probably cleaned it out and given it to someone else by now, but she kept insisting that it would be fine. The fairy holds her hand out, palm up, blows a puff of shimmery green dust over the window, smirks at me over her shoulder, and opens the window. I guess I shouldn't be surprised, but it still startles me to see magic being used.

She ushers me in through the open window. When I step inside, I'm floored. It's like I never left. Everything is in exactly the same place it was when I left. The bed is still made; I can even see the indentation from Aiden's body where he laid the night he took me to Neverland. I can picture it perfectly in my head, see his smirk when I came out of the bathroom, his relaxed position, hands behind his head. My stomach heaves, and I turn away.

"This is where I leave you," Tatiana says. "Enjoy your ordinary life, Elena."

I start to respond, but she's out the window before I can even open my mouth. Hurrying to the window, I lean out just in time to catch sight of a flash of light in the sky. Any ordinary person who sees it will think it's just a shooting star, but I know the truth. I'll never be able to forget it, no matter how hard I try.

I turn back to the empty dorm room, so different from the treehouse on the island, from the Jolly Roger. The modern room seems so alien after spending weeks living on a pirate ship. Turning on the lights, I wander into the living room and settle on the couch. It seems so strange that the school hasn't gotten rid of my stuff yet, hasn't given this room to another student. But considering the fact that my uncle is the headmaster, maybe I shouldn't be so surprised.

Feeling too restless to sit still, to stay in this room, I decide to venture out, to wander the halls, to find out what has changed since I've been gone. Looking down at my clothes, I realize that I haven't changed them since I got back to the Jolly Roger after killing Aiden. Tentatively, I sniff at the sweater draped over my shoulders. It smells like Will, like wind and the sea. Pain grips my heart, crushing it in its fist. I rip the sweater off and toss it to the floor, discard the rest of the clothes as well, and slip into a pair of sweatpants and a hoodie.

Without allowing myself to think of *him*, or of *that place*, I stalk into the hall, slamming the door behind me. I set off toward the front of the building, expecting the Christmas decorations to have been packed away by now. The stale, sour smell of the foyer hits me before I'm halfway down the hallway, and I wrinkle my nose, but continue on.

When I get to the landing at the top of the massive staircase, it all looks the same. The scantily decorated Christmas tree is still in the corner of the foyer, the strings of half burned-out lights are still strung through the banister and around the high ceilings. It's as if no time has passed at all.

Confused and a little freaked out, I wander down the stairs to try to figure out just what has gone on in my absence. The wood of the bannister is smooth under my hand as I descend to the first floor. Around the first corner, light is spilling onto the floor from Uncle Henry's office. I pick up my pace, intending to pass by unnoticed, but after only a few steps, I stop. If anyone has noticed my absence, it will be the headmaster, my uncle, so I turn back and knock lightly on his door.

"Come in," he calls, his voice muffled by the door. I push open the door and slide into the cramped little office. Uncle Henry looks up, his spectacles perched on the bridge of his nose.

"Hello, Elena." He smiles up at me. "Is there something I can help you with?"

Is it really possible that no time has passed here? I wonder as I plaster a smile on my face. "Oh no, Uncle Henry, I just saw your light on and thought I'd check in," I say.

"Good, good. It's been a few days since you arrived; are you settling in nicely?" he asks.

A few days. It's only been a few days.

I try to keep my face blank, neutral. Try to hide the shock that is coursing through my body.

"I'm settling in fine." I force myself to smile. "I'll let you get back to your work though, good night."

I make to slip out of the office, but my uncle's voice stops me.

"Elena?" he calls after me.

I turn and face him, schooling my features into neutrality once more. "Yes?"

"I do hope you haven't been opening your windows, Elena. I would hate for you to catch a chill from this ghastly weather."

The words are innocent enough, but it's the tone of his voice, the knowing look in his eyes that tells me that my uncle knows that it's not just a chill that might come in through those windows…

"Of course not, Uncle Henry," I say, careful to keep the mask on my face, but my voice cracks a little at the end of my sentence, and I hope it doesn't betray my lie. He nods, but his eyes don't leave my face. I hurry out of his office and shut the door behind me, leaning against it while my brain processes the fact that though I've been gone for weeks, only a few days have passed in London. I'm also trying to come to terms with the fact that my uncle might know much, much more than he leads on.

Just another thing that I shouldn't be surprised about, I guess. After all, I did travel to a magical world with Aiden, and met pirates and fairies and mermaids. Shaking my head, I set off again, this time back to my room.

I reach the top of the staircase, still lost in my thoughts, and run right into someone. "I'm so sorry! I wasn't watching where I was going," I say, steadying myself with a hand on the bannister. After a few moments, I realize that the person I just slammed into is familiar.

"No worries," Cash chuckles. "We've got to stop meeting this way though, don't you think?" He smiles, his melted chocolate eyes taking in my messy hair, my hoodie and sweatpants.

A blush burns in my cheeks. "I'm sorry," I repeat, trying to skirt around Cash and escape back to my room.

He blocks my way, leaving me stuck on the top stair, embarrassed and feeling like a slob.

"I should be the one apologizing for how I acted the first time we met," Cash says, his dark eyes almost black in the dim light.

"It's fine, really," I insist, trying again to get around him.

He blocks me again and says, "Let me make it up to you. We should go out, to dinner, or whatever you want."

A ball of ice forms in my stomach. Cash is asking me out… on a date. Will's face flickers to life in my mind, and nausea washes over me. Cash is cute, like, really cute. But I just left Neverland, just left Will, the man I love. Well, loved. It's hard to love someone who ignores you, won't even look at you, who treats you like you're nothing to them. But the thought of dating someone after spending every second with Will is… I can't picture it.

Cash is looking at me expectantly, waiting for an answer, and I have the feeling that he isn't going to take no as that answer. "Alright, deal. I'll let you take me to dinner," I say, a smile plastered on my face to hide the emotional turmoil going on underneath the surface.

"Perfect," he says, his smile stretching wider.

And for the first time, I notice just how attractive his smile is. Maybe going on a date with him won't be so bad, fun even. It might even help me move on.

"I'll meet you here tomorrow at seven?" he asks.

I nod my consent. Cash flashes me one more smile before sauntering off down the hall.

Walking quickly, I make it back to my room and lock myself in. The plain, boring room does nothing to lift my spirits. Out of nowhere, anger starts to build in my chest. Not just anger, *rage*. Rage at Aiden and Tatiana for taking me to Neverland, for tormenting me and trying to kill me. Rage at Will for rescuing me and conning me into falling in love with him, tricking me into giving him all of me, body and soul. For making me feel so deeply for him, for tossing me aside like a dirty shirt, for letting me leave and not coming back with me. The rage builds and builds until it's too much. Dashing to the bedroom, I fling myself onto the rumpled bed, press my face into my pillow, and scream.

I scream as loud as I can, over and over until my throat is raw and burning. The pillow is wet with hot, angry tears. Unable to scream anymore, I roll over. Exhaustion takes me in its claws. I'm tired, so tired.

The captain looks around him at the ship in various states of disarray. He tore apart everything that he could looking for Elena, but she is gone. She left him, and she will never come back. The fire of rage burning inside of him is the only thing keeping the darkness at bay for the time being. He steps over a broken crate, its contents spilled across the floor, and slashes at a net hanging in front of the door, his hook slicing it to ribbons.

His heavy steps echo through the hull as he stalks back up to the main deck. The men he passes jump out of his way and slink into the shadows at the sound of his approach. He must look as enraged as he feels, then. The darkness surges, wrapping itself around his heart and squeezing. But he cannot find it in him to care. Elena is gone, and she is never coming back.

TWENTY ONE

———

When I wake, sunlight is shining through the window. I squeeze my eyes shut against the bright light. Reaching my hand out, I feel for the warm body that I usually find beside me, but Will isn't there. My eyes fly open, and I realize that I am no longer on the Jolly Roger, no longer in Neverland, no longer with Will.

It was so easy to forget about all the bad things that have happened to me recently, especially when my dreams were full of bright blue eyes, the smell of the sea, bare skin on silk sheets. I shake my head. It was just a dream. A dream that will never come true, because I left Neverland, and I am never going back.

Dragging myself out of bed, I find my coffee right where I left it and get a pot brewing. I wander into the bathroom and start to brush my teeth, but the sight of myself in the mirror stops me. My auburn hair is even more wild than it was after the flight home last night, and my eyes have dark circles under them, making the hazel look just a little brighter in contrast.

I decide to shower, not because I care what I look like right now, but because I can still smell Neverland on my skin, in my hair, as if it's a permanent part of me now. I suppose it is a part of me, and always will be. Things happened to me there that I will never be able to forget.

I gave myself to Will, fell in love with him, and had my heart obliterated. I killed Aiden, the magical boy who inspired so many stories and movies from my childhood. I will never be able to forget that those things happened. I will never be able to get them out of my head.

Turning on the shower as hot as it will go, I step in, letting the near scalding water cascade over me, letting it burn away the smells, the feeling of hands on my skin, the feeling of hot blood gushing onto my hand. The water is so hot, but I feel so cold. I find myself wondering if I will ever feel warm again, if I will ever feel love and happiness again.

Then I remember—I agreed to go to dinner with Cash tonight. I cringe without meaning to at the thought of the date. It's not that I don't want to go out with Cash, but… what am I supposed to talk about? Will I be able to pretend that I didn't spend weeks in Neverland, while only days passed here? It will definitely be an interesting dinner.

Sighing, I step out of the shower and wrap myself in a towel. I drag my brush roughly through my hair and go into the other room to pour some coffee without bothering to get dressed. It has been so long since I've had a cup of coffee. The smell of it alone is enough to perk me up some, and I inhale deeply. But even the smell can't compare to the first sip of the hot black liquid. I down the whole cup in record time, refill it, and carry the mug back to the bedroom.

Pulling on an outfit similar to the one I wore to bed last night, I lounge on the soft bed, sipping my coffee, trying to figure out how to get out of this date tonight without being mean, and without having to explain too much. Saying I'm sick is too generic; Cash would probably see through that excuse easily. Nothing good enough is coming to mind, and then there's a soft knock at my door.

I hesitate briefly before crossing through the rooms, but to my relief, I don't even have to open the door. A folded-up piece of paper is lying on the wood floor, my name scrawled across it in distinctly boyish handwriting. I pick it up and open it. The same handwriting is on the inside as well, and the note says, "Hope you like Italian, see you at 7." It isn't signed, but it doesn't need to be. For the first time in what feels like forever, a small smile tugs at my lips.

I study Cash's handwriting, which is messy and slants across the paper at an angle so different from Will's, which was all elegant swirls and swoops. *Stop,* I reprimand myself. *Stop thinking of him. He let you go; now it's time to let him go.* Easier said than done. I've been awake all of an hour, and Will has been on my mind for almost every second of it.

For the millionth time, I wonder if I will ever be able to move on.

The pirate has been drunk for days. Drunk on darkness, rage, and sour wine. What is the point of abstaining now? His brother is dead; there will be no more girls to save, nothing to worry about. He can do as he pleases, go where he chooses, as long as it is in Neverland.

He takes a long gulp from the bottle of wine and tries to stand from his chair, but the room tilts dangerously, so he sinks back down. Oh well, he thinks, no one is missing me anyway.

The pirate takes another swig from his bottle, near empty now, and lets the darkness wash over him.

⁂

I wipe my sweaty palms on my jeans. It's five minutes to seven, and I'm already at the top of the staircase, waiting for Cash. I ran out of stupid excuses not to come before lunchtime, and I felt like if I didn't show up early, I wouldn't show up at all. But that's not part of moving on. So here I am, dressed nicer than I have in weeks, with make-up on my face and my hair done, waiting to go on a date.

I feel ridiculous. But then someone clears their throat behind me, and I turn. Cash is standing there, dressed in a crisp black button-down shirt and dark jeans, holding a single pink rose, his dark eyes shining as he takes me in.

"You look… wow," he says, a smile tugging at one corner of his mouth.

"Thank you." I smile back, amazed at how easy it is. "You look very nice, too."

He holds out the rose, which I take tentatively. My cheeks burn with a blush that I know he can see.

"Shall we?" he asks.

I nod, and he and I walk down the stairs, across the foyer, past the Christmas tree, and out into the cold winter night, side by side

⁂

It has been a week since Elena left, and each day that passes allows more darkness to find its way into the pirate's heart. He has gone through a whole case of wine and a package of pipe tobacco in the days since she left him.

He scratches his chin, now covered in a thick layer of black stubble, and puffs from his pipe. The cabin is filled with so much smoke that

he can barely see the door on the other side of the room. Picking up the wine bottle, he discovers that it is empty. He throws it against the wall, where it shatters into pieces, just like his heart.

The pirate has almost fallen back into his drink-induced stupor, but a bright light fills the room, forcing his eyes open again. He growls at whoever has dared to disturb him and receives a girlish giggle in return. He sits up, blue eyes scanning the room, which is once again dark.

"Elena? Is that you?" he rasps, ashamed at the hope in his voice. The darkness squeezes his heart a little tighter. A reminder that he is no longer in control of his own actions, his own emotions.

"No, pirate," a silvery voice replies. "Elena is gone."

Tatiana steps out from the shadows and the thick cloud of smoke, a sly grin on her face. "You do not look well, Captain," she says.

"How dare you show your face, fairy!" the pirate hisses through clenched teeth, his hands braced on his desk to keep from falling over.

"I do not recall doing anything to bring on such anger," she says, strolling around the dark room, her green eyes on his face.

"You took her away from me. You took Elena from this ship, and now I will never see her again," he snarls.

"She wanted to go, pirate. She asked me to take her out of this place. She was very distraught, so I just assumed that you were done with her." The fairy shrugs.

"I will never be done with her," he says, sinking back into his chair and taking a long drag from his pipe. "Why are you here, fairy? If it is just to taunt me, then you may as well just leave. Being in my own head is torment enough."

Tatiana continues to roam about the room, picking things up and setting them down, running her slender fingers over his possessions. "I came to help you, pirate. After delivering Elena to her home in London, I had a feeling that things were not alright."

"And what can you do to help me, fairy?" Will snaps. "If you are not going to bring Elena back to me, then I have no use for you."

"And what if I told you that I could take you to her?" the fairy asks, her eyes glittering despite the lack of light.

"Then I would tell you the same thing that I told her. That world is no place for a one-handed pirate."

The fairy looks him over, at his disheveled clothing, his lank, unwashed hair, his stubble covered face. He does not care. The darkness squeezes his heart again. A warning.

"I can provide you with what you need to blend in; I can even solve the problem of your missing hand. You can see her again, William," Tatiana says.

I can see her again, the pirate thinks. The darkness inside of him is roiling, squeezing, trying to keep its control.

"I can sense it, you know," the fairy says. "The darkness. I can sense it. Would you like me to rid you of it?"

The pirate opens his mouth, but no words come out. It's as if the darkness has tied his tongue into a knot. Its grip tightens on his heart. Please. Please rid me of this curse! he screams silently, hoping that the fairy can sense his words like she senses his curse. If she cannot help him with her magic, no one can. And he fears that if he is not freed from this prison soon, there will be nothing left of him to free.

"This will not be pleasant, pirate," Tatiana warns. "A darkness such as this tends to fight back."

Will tries to nod, but his head will not move. The darkness is in a frenzy now. Clawing, biting, tearing. Trying to weave itself into him, into his blood, his heart, his mind, his soul.

The fairy nods. "Let us begin."

TWENTY TWO

Cash takes me to a little Italian restaurant only a few blocks from the school. It's so small that there are only eight tables inside, but it's beautiful. Every table is covered by a crisp white tablecloth. Tea lights in pretty votives adorn each table. The dim candlelight makes the place feel very intimate.

Awkward, that's how I feel right now. Awkward, nervous, haunted. The candles, the low light, the small room with shiny wooden floors—it's like I'm back in Will's cabin on the Jolly Roger, back in Aiden's treehouse. I can feel panic stirring inside me, threatening to ruin the evening by bubbling over. The last thing I need now is a panic attack. Explaining that the restaurant reminds me of being in a place that the rest of the world believes to be fictional might be tough.

"Are you alright?" Cash asks, a crease forming between his eyebrows.

No, I think. "Yeah. I'm fine," I say. I force myself to take a few deep breaths, reminding myself that I am not in Neverland, that I'm here, in London, and everything is fine. The panic fades enough for me to put a smile on my face and peruse the menu. It stays subdued long enough to order, to have a normal conversation with Cash while we wait for our food.

The food is amazing. It's the best thing I've eaten in a long time. After weeks of eating mostly dried meat, fish, fruit, and bland bread, my stomach welcomes the filling pasta smothered in flavorful sauce and fresh herbs. I finish my food before Cash is even halfway done with his. He gapes at me across the table. I look down at the tablecloth to hide the blush burning in my cheeks.

"I didn't eat today," I say, not meeting the dark eyes I can feel on my face, burning holes in my façade.

"You don't have to explain yourself," Cash says gently. "I'm just surprised. Most girls don't eat like that. They order a salad and push it around with their forks while making eyes across the table."

I laugh. I laugh, and it feels so… good. Foreign, after so many days spent deep in my own despair, but good. Once I start, I can't stop. Not until tears are running down my face and my stomach hurts. Across the table, Cash is watching me, a look of amusement mixed with something else on his face. I find myself thinking that this feels right. This is what I should be doing. I'm seventeen. I should be dating and laughing and having fun. Not sailing the Never Sea with a crew of pirates, not flying around Neverland and dancing with the fairies. Not killing boys with beautiful green eyes.

For the first time since leaving Neverland, I feel like maybe, just maybe, I didn't make a mistake when I left.

The pirate grits his teeth against the pain. It's been hours, maybe even days, since the fairy known as Tatiana started the process of extracting the darkness from his body. It has fought back the entire time, is still fighting. Slowly, one inky black tendril at a time, she pulls it from deep within him and casts it into the fire burning in the brazier in the corner.

"Only fire can truly get rid of the darkness," she told him before she began.

He had known this would not be a painless process, but nothing had prepared him for the agony he is experiencing now. But with each wisp she pulls from him, his head gets a bit clearer, his heart beats a bit more freely. It is not only physical pain that he feels, though. As his mind clears, he realizes more and more just what a massive mistake he made when he cast Elena aside. His Elena, beautiful, vibrant, strong, and gone.

"Not much longer now," the fairy murmurs. She closes her eyes and places her hand, hot and glowing with magic, over his heart. Its pace quickens at her touch, at the anticipation of what is to come. The darkness claws at his insides, trying to hold on, shrieking. Or maybe the screams are coming from him. He does not know.

Aside from my almost-panic attack and laughing fit at dinner, the evening has gone surprisingly well. After leaving the restaurant, we walked around for a while, talking and looking at the lights and Christmas decorations. Before I went to Neverland, I wouldn't have found them as beautiful as I do tonight. I was dreading spending the holiday alone in a place I barely knew. But now, less than a week until Christmas, I feel a little bit... excited.

Maybe I won't have to spend it alone in my dorm room; maybe I can spend it sipping hot cocoa next to a fire with the cute, sweet guy next to me.

Cash and I take our time walking back to school, admiring the brightly lit shop windows full of toys and clothes and holiday paraphernalia. We even go into one of the shops and browse for a while. Looking at the bright, shiny ornaments, I find myself wishing that I had a miniature Christmas tree in my room to hang some on.

I turn to tell Cash my thoughts, only to find that he isn't behind me like I thought. My heart lurches into a gallop, and I have to brace myself against the wall, force my breathing to slow, tell myself that this isn't Neverland. There isn't any danger.

"Elena?" a voice says from behind me. "Are you sure you're alright?"

I plaster the too-big smile on my face before turning to face Cash. "Of course," I reply. "I thought I felt a migraine coming on, but I'm fine now." He nods, but the look of concern and wariness on his face tells me that he doesn't believe my lies. Smart boy. I let him lead me out of the shop and back into the cold. We don't talk much the rest of the way home.

The smell of the foyer hits me like a ton of bricks when Cash opens the door, and I gag.

"You never quite get used to it," he says with a knowing smile.

I make for the staircase, eager to go anywhere that smells better, but his voice stops me.

"Elena, wait. I—I have something to give you."

I turn, and sure enough, in his hand is a small brown paper bag. My cheeks grow warm, but I cross the space to stand in front of him. He hands me the paper bag, and when I see what's inside, I forget to breathe for a few seconds. I reach in and gently pull out the ornament—a delicate silver snowflake crusted with glittering, diamond-like stones. Letting it hang by its string from my finger, I hold it up, marveling at each intricate detail, at the way the light catches the stones and casts rainbows across the dark wood floor.

"It's beautiful," I say, my voice breathy and soft. "Thank you."

Cash smiles. "I saw you eyeing the ornaments in the shop and thought you might like one of your own."

"I love it. But I don't have anywhere to hang it."

He sucks his lower lip into his mouth, thinking, then glances behind him at the sad-looking Christmas tree. "I think that tree could use a little extra beauty, don't you?" he asks.

I feel the smile spread wide across my face as I nod. Carrying the silver snowflake, I make my way over to the tree, circle it, and find the perfect spot to hang it: right in front, where the light will catch the stones. "Perfect," I say, turning back to Cash.

"Yes," he says, admiring the new addition to the tree. "It is."

For the second time tonight, I find myself thinking that I made the right decision leaving Neverland.

We climb the stairs side by side, neither of us feeling the need to fill the peaceful silence with forced conversation. On the second-floor landing, Cash faces me and says, "I had a good time. Thank you for gracing me with your presence this evening." His playful smile is enough to bring a smile to my face, too.

"Thank you for inviting me out," I say, leaning against the bannister. "I needed this."

Cash's eyes travel from my eyes down to my lips, and I know what he's going to do even before he leans in. My thoughts go wild. Do I let him kiss me? Do I stop him? Do I run away and avoid him for the rest of my time here?

I put a hand on his chest, stopping him before he can get too close. "I have to tell you something," I say. He straightens, his smile gone. "It's not that I didn't enjoy myself, and it's not that I don't *want* to. But—but I just got out of a pretty serious relationship, and I think we should probably take this slow." I feel ridiculous for saying the words, but I had to explain it to him somehow. Because even though I think he can help me move on, I can't bear for him to kiss me. Not yet. *Maybe not ever.*

Cash's face softens, his smile returning. "I understand," he says gently. "I would never try to make you do something you aren't ready for."

"Thank you," I say, stretching up on my toes and kissing him lightly on the cheek. "I really did have a good time tonight. Good night, Cash." I turn and walk back to my room without looking back.

"Good night, Elena," he calls after me.

Back at my room, I unlock the door and step inside, still thinking about the pretty snowflake ornament now hanging on a branch downstairs. Dropping my purse on the floor, I wander over to the coffee maker, wondering if I will sleep at all tonight if I drink a cup. The smell hits me harder than the sour, stale foyer below. Salt, wind, smoke, wine.

"You look lovely, Elena."

The voice that comes from behind me stops my heart. Rough like sandpaper, but with a lilting accent that makes it sound elegant. I don't even have to turn around to know who it belongs to. I knew he was here just by the smell. *Will.*

TWENTY THREE

Will is here, in my dorm room, in London. The memories I had managed to push away for a few hours come flooding back. Every kiss, every touch, every word. It's like my heart is shattering all over again. I can't look at him. I won't. He tossed me aside and acted like I was nothing to him. So why is he here now?

"Say something, love. Anything. Just look at me," Will pleads.

Love. He called me love, just like before. My hands ball into tight fists at my sides. How can he call me that after what he did to me? "Why are you here, Will?" I ask without turning. I can hear the anger in my voice, but I don't care. He deserves every angry word. He deserves to stand there while I refuse to look at him. Just like he did to me.

"Please, love. I can explain," he says.

I cut him off before he can get another word out. Whirling around, I unleash all of my suppressed rage, all of my pain. "Explain what? Explain why you treated me like dirt? Why you tossed me aside and ignored me? Why you refused to listen when I *begged* you to come here with me? Why are you here, Will? Is this some kind of sick joke, a game you're trying to play? Because I am *done!*"

I didn't notice when I started crying, but sure enough, hot tears are rolling down my cheeks, dropping to the floor. It's too much. This is all too much. I don't think I can handle any more. My legs give out beneath me, and I crumple to the floor. And then Will is there, gathering me into his arms, wiping the tears away. My knight in shining armor. My hero.

"I didn't want to do any of those things. Please believe me, Elena. I wanted to come with you. I wanted to tell you how much I love you, that I want this life with you. Please believe me," he says, his breath warm on my neck.

"Then why did you say no? Why did you break me into a million pieces and let me think you didn't care?" I ask, my voice barely a whisper.

"Because I was broken into a million pieces too, Elena. Because there was a darkness in me that saw an opportunity to take control, and I wasn't strong enough to stop it."

"There was a darkness in you? What does that even mean?" I demand.

So, he launches into a story. A dark, twisted story that he never told me in our time together in Neverland. A story about two brothers who were willing to do anything to avoid being drafted into war. How they made a wish on a falling star one night, a wish that was heard by the fairy shooting through the sky.

He tells me about how the fairy granted their wish and flew

them to Neverland, about the early days the brothers spent there together. I let him hold me in his arms and tell me that when they decided to stay in Neverland permanently, there was a deal they had to strike with the fairies. Because Neverland was not a place they were supposed to stay in, it was meant to be a place that children travelled to in their dreams, a place that disappeared when they woke up.

In order to stay in Neverland, in order to age slowly enough that they would stay young for many, many years, both brothers had to give up a piece of their soul. What they didn't know was that the piece that was taken from them was replaced by darkness. A trick played on them by the fairies, who did not want them to remain in Neverland. The fairies believed that the darkness would destroy them, or that they would use it to destroy each other.

The brothers struggled against the darkness for a long time, kept it buried deep, until the day that one brother decided it wasn't enough to age slowly—he didn't want to age at all. He went to the fairies and demanded that they give him magic. Magic that would allow him to fly, to do whatever he wanted to do and make him never age. So, they did. The fairies granted him the magic he desired, and told him how to steal the years from others and use them to stay young.

Will tells me about how Aiden came to him and showed him his new powers, told him about his plan to steal years and never age again. Will didn't agree with Aiden's plan. He was content to age slowly, to be able to spend multiple lifetimes sailing across Neverland. This made Aiden angry, so he banned Will from the island.

When Aiden brought Wendy to the island, Will tried to save her from his brother, and he thought he had. But when Wendy was killed, Will broke just enough that the darkness lingering inside of him was able to take hold. Since that day, it has been a constant struggle to keep it at bay, to keep it from taking root in his heart and ruining him forever.

Will tells me that the night I killed Aiden and asked Tatiana to take me home, he broke enough to allow the darkness to take root. That it surged and grew until he couldn't fight it anymore, until he didn't have control over his own actions. He tells me about how Tatiana pulled it from his heart, one agonizing tendril at a time, and then brought him here, to me.

For a few minutes after he finishes his story, I don't speak. I just chew on my bottom lip and let everything he told me really sink in. Will stays silent as well, watching my face, letting me take the time that I need. A thousand questions are swirling around inside my skull, and I need to figure out which are the most important to ask.

"All that time we spent together in Neverland… why didn't you tell me about the darkness?" I ask first.

"Because I thought I had it under control. And because I love you, Elena. I am already flawed enough; I didn't want to add to the already long list of reasons why you should not love me back," he says, his bright eyes burning into mine.

Fair enough. "If the fairies are the ones who gave Aiden his magic, why was he able to control them?" I ask next.

"An oversight on their part. They granted him powerful magic so that our destruction would come sooner. If one brother had magic, and the other did not, they thought that at least one brother would end up dead, and that they could deal with the other. Instead, they granted him so much magic that he was able to use it to control them, and he forced them to do his bidding from the moment he found out he could, until the moment he died."

The rest of the story I've heard before. I know what happened to Wendy. "What happened to the Jolly Roger when you left Neverland?"

Will smiles and says, "I thought it was time she had a new captain. Captain Miles."

I return his smile, picturing the massive man at the wheel, barking orders. I think Mr. Miles will do just fine in his new position. All my other questions seem pointless now. All except one. "So, you really do love me?" I ask, looking down at my hands.

Will lifts my chin and leans in so close that our breath mixes, his eyes never leaving mine. "Yes, Elena. I love you. And I will keep loving you until I draw my last breath."

I can't wait any longer. Crushing my mouth to his, I breathe him in, the smell of salt water and wind mixed with smoke and the heady scent of his favorite sour wine. I run my hands all over him, up his arms, across his broad, strong shoulders, along his jaw, thick with black stubble. He's really here. This isn't just a dream.

Will runs his hands up my back, through my hair, touching my face. I pull back, gasping for air, and take his wrists in my hands. The gleaming silver hook is gone, and in its place is a black leather glove, complete with five fingers.

He laughs softly. "You can thank Tatiana for that if you ever see her again. It may not be a real, working hand, but it will blend in a bit easier here."

Looking him over, I realize that Tatiana provided him with modern clothes as well. He's wearing black jeans, a white t-shirt, and a black leather jacket, but on his feet are the same pair of worn leather boots that he has worn every day that I've known him, and for much longer than that, I'm sure. Now, instead of looking like a pirate, he looks like a guy who would ride up to a bar on the back of a motorcycle.

"Do I look alright?" he asks, looking down at the foreign clothes. "I'm not quite sure that the fairy—"

But I don't let him finish his sentence. Practically tackling him, I kiss him, deeply and for a very long time. When we finally come up for air, Will props himself up on an elbow.

"I take it that you haven't forgotten about me and moved on

with that boy I saw you walk in with, then?" he asks, a playful smile tugging at his lips.

Cash. He saw me with Cash. I forgot all about him the second I found Will in my room. It was only one date, but it's going to be awful telling Cash that I won't be going out with him again. And the snowflake! The beautiful silver snowflake that he bought for me. I feel like a complete and total jerk. But… it was just one date. Do I even need to give him an explanation? *Oh well, I think, I can figure all of that out later.*

"It's you, Will. From the moment I opened my eyes on your ship and saw your face. It was you then, it's you now, and it will always be you," I say before I cover his mouth with mine and let myself melt into him.

EPILOGUE

High above the city of London, *the fairy known as Tatiana perches on the edge of a cloud, looking down at the glimmering lights.*

"Well done, Tatiana."

The fairy turns and looks at the boy with the strange green eyes, a savage smile stretched across her face. "I should be the one congratulating you. You are the one who so convincingly died in that cave."

The boy reclines on the fluffy white cloud. "Yes, I was very convincing, wasn't I? But your magic is what brought me back."

"We make a good team," the fairy says, gazing at the boy with admiration and longing in her eyes.

"Yes, we make a very clever pair indeed," he says, smiling up at the stars.

The fairy flits over to the boy and seats herself upon his chest. "What will happen now?" she asks him.

The boy takes the tiny fairy in his hand before sitting up, his eyes fixing on the spot far below, where he knows his brother and his queen are having a very happy reunion. "Now," he says, his eyes sparkling with excitement. "Let the games begin."

About the Author

Nicole Knapp is originally from California, currently living in Oklahoma. She loves to read and write Young Adult Romance, fantasy, and the classics. The Missing Piece is available from Amazon in paperback and Kindle version. Hook & Crown, a dark and twisted retelling of Peter Pan, is set to release in Autumn 2019 from Parliament House Publishing.

facebook.com / AuthorNicoleKnapp

Aiden, Elena, & Will Need Your Help!

Did you enjoy *Hook & Crown*? Reviews keep books alive . . .

Aiden, Elena, and Will still need you! Help them by leaving your review on either GoodReads or the digital storefront of your choosing.

Thank you!